Our Overtime

ICE LEAGUE BOOK 1

S.C. Kate

To my amazing, crazy, fun family

To my brothers for playing some great hockey, and to my sisters for being the best beta readers

1 JULES- 15 YEARS AGO

I didn't know if I was allowed to say yes to him… And I still couldn't believe he asked me.

He worked in the front office of the rink, punching our ice time cards whenever we went out for a practice session. He only worked a couple days a week. I knew this was because he was probably one of the many guys who lived with a billet family and played on the junior team here at the Ice League and worked for discounted ice time.

But I thought he'd been watching my friend, a term I used loosely for her, named Ally, not me.

I was too shy to even look at him when I handed my punch card over. Ally was the one who had conversations with him. If I said one word in the conversation, I was thinking about how stupid I sounded for the rest of the day, so I usually just stayed quiet.

He was one of those funny, magnetic kinds of people, like everything he said was meant to make someone smile and everyone loved him. I was envious of those kinds of people because no matter how hard I tried it didn't seem like anyone ever wanted to stick around me for very long. I hadn't even seen my grandparents who I lived with in about two weeks.

I walked down the rubber-floored hallway to the front office to punch my card a little earlier than usual today. Another girl I skated with was having a breakdown in the locker room and I wanted out.

I'd rather hang in the lobby than be pulled into that drama.

I didn't realize he was in the office alone until it was too late to walk away. I would look awkward as hell if I did that. I took a shaky breath and handed my card over, reminding myself I'd be on the safety of the ice in five minutes. He lifted his head and gave a bright smile and his whole face up to his eyes seemed to light up.

I thought the whole exchange was going to happen without words until he suddenly spoke.

"Hullo again. What's your name?" he said in what I detected as a slight Canadian accent.

I felt awkward under his gaze and paused a second too long, "Uh, Julianna…Hurley," I stammered out. "Yours?"

"Makes sense," he said, nodding seriously, and pushing a hand through his short brown hair.

"Huh?"

"Pretty girl, pretty name," he said with his head tilted to the side as he studied me. "I feel like I've heard Hurley before," he tapped his fingers thinking. "Do you have any brothers who play?"

I felt my face blush hot at his compliment and tried to focus on what he was saying past that. "Play?" I asked.

"The best sport," he said with confidence, puffing out his chest, "Hockey."

"Oh," I hesitated not knowing how much I should share with a stranger. "My dad… uh…"

Realization dawned on his face and his eyebrows scrunched together. "I'm sorry, Julianna, I didn't realize... I just-" he stammered for a second, and I felt the upper hand and eagerness to help him out of the uncomfortableness of the situation.

"It's ok, I don't remember at all," I grimaced with the slight embarrassment I always felt over not remembering my father's death, which I knew in the back of my mind was a misplaced feeling. It wasn't unusual for people not to remember before the age of four, I'd looked it up enough times to be sure, but it never soothed the guilt for some reason. My father was a hockey star, I was told. He'd reached the NHL and played for the Rangers for two complete seasons. In the midst of his third season, he had a heart attack on the ice and never made it home to me. All I had of our father-daughter bond were a couple of photos: Him holding toddler me up on the ice after a conference championship game, and him proudly smiling with me sitting inside the coveted Stanley cup.

I guess I also had his parents, who raised me as well. He left them, however, with no information on my mother, an aspect I knew they were salty about. After being shut down at each point of questioning pertaining to my mother, I left the subject, but gathered the fact that they believed that with "all of the women throwing themselves at hockey players," she was "just another puck bunny," according to my grandmother. I had a hard time believing this because I couldn't even talk to boys usually.

My grandparents didn't understand my need to be on the ice, considering where his death took place and all, and if I ever asked to play hockey, I think they'd both have aneurysms. But I always chalked that up as another tally in my mental column of the ways they didn't really know me. The rink was the only place I felt closer to knowing something about him; and at least they respected the sport of figure skating.

I felt the need to change the subject and push pity away. "Well, what's your name?"

"Greyson Scott. But I go by Grey," he added with a wink.

It was my turn to study him. It was a strong, but serious name. He didn't seem like a serious guy to me. Maybe he'd grow into it one day… but that would be kind of a shame. I liked his lightness.

"So, Julianna, you ever skate at Tenny Park?"

The question took me by surprise. "Uh, no. I love outdoor skating, but I don't get to go much," I admitted.

"You love outdoor skating and you've never been to Tenny?!" He asked, acting aghast at the idea.

My face heated again, and I felt my lips twist in amusement. "I've always wanted to," I pointed out, "But I'd probably get in trouble for skating out there."

"In trouble?" He asked curiously.

"Yeah, because I have to practice every day. I'd have to skate there at night, and then somehow get my skates sharpened and ready to go for the next day."

He nodded, "Because it kind of trashes your blades. I usually use old skates," he said simply.

"I give 'em away," I replied lamely.

"What? What if you become a famous figure skater? You just gave away skates people would fight over!"

He said it as if it were the end of the world and I couldn't tell if he was joking or not, but I laughed at his reaction and shook my head, "I'm not going to be famous."

His eyes popped out and he looked at me like I was crazy. I felt myself get a little defensive until he said, "I've seen you out there, Jules. You're pretty fucking great."

Two thoughts popped into my mind almost simultaneously- I liked the way he said Jules. No one called me that. And he'd seen me skate? That really made my face hot. I wished I could turn off my self-consciousness. I couldn't comprehend why he would watch me. This cute boy. Watched me? I tugged at the hole in my gloves and couldn't look back at him.

"You could always drive to have them sharpened before practice the next day?" He suggested with a shrug. His shoulders were so much stronger and broader than mine, he practically looked like he had shoulder pads on.

"I can't drive," I said a little too quickly. I was shocked at how fast I was finding words. I usually couldn't converse with boys, but of course I could talk just long enough to offer up an embarrassing fact about myself.

He looked at me strangely then. It was true though. I was already 16, so I should've been able to, but my grandparents never had time to teach me, and I was pretty busy myself anyways. All my hours were dedicated to school or skating. I rode the bus to school. The rink was across the street from the high school. And then I rode the bus home. It was pretty simple, and I was fine with it.

"Let's make a deal," he said. His eyebrows scrunched together in fake concentration. "What if we go to Tenny Park tonight and skate, and then I'll sharpen your skates before your practice tomorrow? I'm getting pretty good at it, and I can do it for free. Tomorrow's Saturday, so you get here at 9, right?"

I ignored the second part, of course he knew figure skating hours because he worked here, not because he had specifically watched me… right? I focused on what really blew my mind, "You want to go to Tenny Park... with me?" I asked, I couldn't keep the skepticism out of my voice. I was hesitant to say yes in case he was just trying to make fun of me. Why would this unbelievably cute boy want to take me out skating? I'd never been asked out on a date before… did this qualify as a date? I'm pretty sure it did…

"Yes," he said firmly.

"Uh.. why?"

"Because I want to hold your hand," he said with a confident look on his face. "And maybe kiss you," he wagged his eyebrows at me. "And I've wanted to ask you out for a long time," he smiled.

I opened my mouth, but no words came. I'd never kissed anyone before. I found it hard to swallow; it felt like I'd achieved a whole new level of nervousness.

"So, I can drive. You punched in for two hours, so you leave here around 5ish, so I'll pick you up at 6:30ish?"

It was a good thing he kept talking, because I was too shocked to come up with words… so I gave him a swift nod.

We were going skating. I didn't want to dress up. That would be dumb, I told myself. I stressed over what I was wearing anyway. I decided on black leggings, gray leg warmers, and my light blue warm-up jacket. It would be kind of chilly, but I didn't want to wear a ton of layers and look all puffy. I wished I had a friend to run this by, but I usually kept to myself. At the rink, everyone was a competitor first, friend only second. I berated myself for not getting closer to anyone now though. Why wasn't I more social? Then I wouldn't be so weird. I debated putting my hair up or down for the last half hour and decided to leave it down. He'd never seen it down before because it was always pinned in my signature low bun for skating. I decided I'd bring a ponytail in case I wanted to jump or spin and needed to tie my hair up.

The doorbell cut off my thoughts. Well, I guess if I blew it, I wouldn't have to tell anyone.

I quickly ran downstairs and opened the door to reveal The Boy. The very first boy who asked me out. He looked even more cute in his hockey warm up pants and a team sweatshirt, and he perfected the messy but nice look with his dark hair.

"Damn, this is a huge house," Grey said, as he looked around the foyer. He finally rested his eyes on me, and I immediately felt my cheeks burn. He reached out to tug the ends of my hair. "You look lovely, Miss Jules." It seemed he had decided on that nickname, and it made me feel warm inside. No one had ever given me a nickname before.

"Huge, but no one ever in it. The house," I joked, but it didn't come off as funny as I'd meant it to, and it left me feeling too transparent. I just wanted to turn his hot gaze away from me. Grey bit his cheek in and just nodded, like he understood what I was saying.

I grabbed my skating bag and following him out the door to his old truck.

"So, I was gonna take you to a fancy dinner, but I like really really love the pizza at Old Tenny's concession stand... Annnd I only have like 10 dollars to my name right now. That okay?" He grinned as he climbed into his truck.

"That sounds perfect," I felt myself relax a bit into the lumpy seat.

"You gonna be warm enough in that?" He asked genuinely, looking at me with a doubtful face.

"Yeah, I'm used to the cold. I won't complain," I told him, but I was questioning my wardrobe choice.

He reached behind him and grabbed another team sweatshirt from his back bench seat and handed it to me with a wink.

"I gotcha covered. You're a tiny thing, you'll freeze out there without it."

I'd never worn a guy's sweatshirt before. I felt a mixture of shock and giddiness over it and was immediately met with its strong woodsy mixed with clean laundry scent. I wondered if that was just him or some kind of guy cologne he used. Whatever it was, I wanted to bottle it up because it really put my candles to shame. I wondered if they sold "boy" scented ones.

I looked down at it in my lap and noticed that printed in big capitals was the name Scott and under it read #29.

"My birthday is the 29th," I told him, and then internally slapped myself for saying something so dumb, like that was something we had in common or something.

But he didn't make fun of me or act weird over it. He just gave me a bright smile. "My lucky number."

At Tenny Park, we sat on a bench together and laced up our skates.

"I always tie up my left skate first," he told me. "It's my one superstition… that and my lucky undies," he joked.

I arched an eyebrow at him, "You really have lucky undies?"

Red entered his cheeks, and I was shocked that this human actually got embarrassed, I was thinking it didn't happen to him. He had a way of always seeming so sure of himself, I was envious of it.

"Change of subject," he said. "You have any superstitions?"

"I do," I confirmed. "I have to warm up the exact same every day. And I have to do my double axel in the exact same spot every time. It drives my coach crazy."

"Where's that?"

"On the bleacher side of the blue line. The blue line furthest from the zam doors. I set up with crossovers kind of loosely around center ice."

He nodded and regarded me with a look that said he was impressed, "Now every time I'm running drills by that spot, I'll think of you landing a triple axel right there for me," he smiled.

I rolled my eyes, "yeah, triple axel, sure," I joked. "Because like three girls in the whole world can do that."

"Well, whatever you do out there is pretty damn impressive to me."

"I can't believe you've watched our side," I said.

"I don't watch your side, I watch you," he pointed out.

Those words really took me for a loop. I guess he could see the surprise on my face, because he let out a chuckle.

He looked out to the ice that stretched before us then. "I really love it out here," he said. "Like a lot more than the regular rink. When I'm old I'm going to build a huge rink in my backyard." He made a gesture with his arms to emphasize how big he wanted it. "I'll have all my friends over and have a huge tournament party."

"That sounds fun," I mused. I couldn't help but think of how different we were. I wouldn't have anyone to invite. But I guess that could be the difference between playing a sport with friends versus going against them. "I love it out here too. This is much more fun. No pressure." My eyes followed a little girl struggling to chase boys in hockey skates.

He turned to me, and I felt his gaze on my cheek.

"You feel pressure on the ice?" he asked in a surprised tone.

"Don't you?"

He shook his head, "it's my release of pressure." He stood then and started gliding away from me. "Stick with me Ju-ju and I'll teach you my ways," he winked.

Skating with him was a different kind of fun. I didn't get the triumphant feeling I usually did when I landed jumps or executed perfect spins. I was just having fun doing fancy footwork next to him, and then he'd try to replicate it, usually failing miserably and causing me to crack up laughing. It was probably the most I'd laughed in a long time. Every once in a while, I'd go off and throw a simple axle or double loop- the only jumps I felt comfortable enough to do in front of him because I felt confident that I wouldn't fall on them. He applauded every time, making me feel special, even though I'd been doing those jumps since I was probably seven and they weren't very impressive. I cherished the feeling of how deep my blades cut into the iced over river. I really had always wanted to skate here.

Tenny Park consisted of a river that ran through the city, so a couple times we skated under bridges that cars crossed over. As we crossed under an impressive looking bridge, I pulled myself into a quick layback spin, amazed at the cool sound of the echo the cars were making above me.

Still a little dizzy, I glided back to an awestruck Grey.

"You're like art," he said when I reached him.

"What?" I asked, laughing at the notion.

"Yeah, it's like you're so seamless. There's no stop and start like hockey, it's just one beautiful, ever-moving painting," he said with admiration in his voice.

He was quite taller than me, but I could tell looking up into his eyes that they were serious. They were beautiful, kind eyes, deep brown and rimmed in red from the cold, with the most impressive eyelashes I'd ever seen.

"Thank you," I told him, earnestly. No one had ever been that complimentary of my skating.

"I feel like you don't even get it," He joked.

"Huh?" I asked confusedly.

He stopped, reached out to grab my hand, and then tugged me back towards him.

"God, I love that. Any other girl would've fallen on her ass," he said. He pulled me into a tight, warm hug and looked down at me.

"You have the prettiest, and bluest eyes I have ever seen." He looked unsure of himself for the first time then. "Can I kiss you?"

Excited nerves coursed through my body, and I felt myself nod.

He slowly angled his head near mine, and touched my lips briefly, and then lingered. His lips were so warm and soft. I wanted more, and I think he sensed so. He pushed down firmer then, and my lips parted for his tongue. He swept it through my mouth and then playfully bit my lower lip.

When he lifted his head, I was immediately nervous. Did I do it right? I wanted to do it again, but did he?

"Damn," he gave me a quick squeeze and rested his chin on my head. "Fuckin fireworks, Juju."

I couldn't help but let a happy little giggle escape.

When I got to the rink the next day, my skates were waiting in the locker room with a note scrawled in crappy boy handwriting: "I had a really great time Juju. Wanna grab donuts with me and the boys after practice today? They wanna meet my girl. And don't worry about the damn bus. I'll be giving you a ride."

Was I already his girl? We'd only had one date, but by the end of it, it felt like we'd known each other for much longer. He was kind. He was exuberant. He was brilliant. The kind of person you wanted to be around. The kind of person you hoped to God really liked you.

And I really did want a donut and to meet his friends.

I felt suddenly seen and wanted. And I wanted more than anything for him to kiss me again.

2 GREY-PRESENT

I watched her move up the metal stands of the rink. She's still a tiny, bow-legged thing, but her waist and legs look slimmer than they did at 22. She's less girlish and less muscular now, but she still moves with a sense of grace, like she always had.

I remember asking her if she thought she was a princess once, definitely drunk at the time, but she couldn't help but move that way. I was always in awe of her. She was naturally pure gentleness, and she was trained in grace through her skating days; days that I'd been a part of.

I studied her long, light brown hair tucked under a baseball hat; it gathered in a low pony, and tumbled down her back, ending lighter at the bottom. It's a lot longer than when I'd last seen it, but it still had a wave to it. Without even seeing the front of the cap, I knew it was probably a piece of old NY Rangers memorabilia with frayed edges, a hand-me-down from her late father. She could have walked right out of a memory, and that notion all but froze my fucking heart.

The only thing out of place was the fancy coat she wore. It didn't match the hat and Nikes, nor the girl that I once knew under the coat. Unless she changed just that much.

I tried to do the math in my head… it'd been about nine years I think since I last saw her walk away from me. Everything about the way she moved and looked was unique, and I'd know it was her walking away from me anywhere, any day.

I'd bet a grand she had no clue that I was standing on the ice below her. I shook my head and blew out a breath of cold air. What a joke. Below. Her. Two words that made sense when it came to the two of us.

God. I needed to get her out of my head. This was supposed to be enjoyable for me, but her presence developed a twisted knot of regret, self-pity, and pure hatred in my very core- hate for her, hate for myself.

I closed my eyes and felt the cool air gently blowing against my face and absorbed in the hum of the rink around me. So, she got pregnant the same year she left me… Well, that hurt.

Nope, don't even go there, man, I told myself.

I tried turning my focus to breathing and looking straight ahead, but the urge to see her again was too strong. I wanted to look at her. No, more. I wanted to look her in the eye and make her see how she left me…

Nope.

I needed to stop this.

To stop thinking.

The kids would be filing onto the ice soon. It didn't matter that she was here. Not at all. I hadn't thought of her in years. Why would I start now?

But that was the lie I always told myself. She was the reason every one of my drunk hookups were always with short brunette girls. She was never too far off my mind's radar.

I felt my chest constricting and I squatted down against it to stretch out my legs.

So what? It'd be an hour that we were in the same place. She was somewhere out there in the world living her life every day, something I bitterly reminded myself of often when I was young and we first separated. I had a hat on, and I'd pull it lower. I'd ignore her son. And I'd have to cut her son. Just as long as I'd be able to figure out his last name.

I couldn't bear to watch her in the stands every game knowing and thinking about the past. Seeing her with a husband would possibly make me mentally and physically ill. Just thinking about it brought bile to my throat. How could it not? For years I had thought- no, was sure- that I'd be her husband.

But we were just kids when I thought that. Why the fuck did it matter at all? It didn't.

Damnit. I forced my dry mouth to choke down a swallow as I viewed her under the brim of my hat. Why did she have to look so small up there in the bleachers?

Only her presence could cause so much confusion, making me feel so utterly and fucking alone, but wanting to shelter her at the same time. Wanting to scream at her, but also ask why? Why not me?

I felt something tap the back of my leg pulling me out of my trance.

"Greys, man," Max laughed at me. "Y'alright there, bud? Ya look a bit shooken up."

For a split-second I thought about asking him if he knew she was up there, but I hesitated. I didn't want him thinking that I cared at all. He had definitely been watching me a second before though, because he turned his head to where I had just been looking. I held my breath, waiting for him to realize.

"Hockey moms, man," He revealed his toothless smile. He didn't notice. Max should be smiling about hockey moms. He was exactly their type. Having the appearance of a professional athlete, but one who just missed the NHL, making him reachable in their eyes. He was the perfect mix of tough looking, with a missing tooth, slightly crooked nose, and a face that was never clean shaven, which paired perfectly with his boyish, goofy demeanor. The women flocked to him. I, on the other hand, having played a bit in the NHL, had no luck with women, and didn't want any either. I used up my luck and I didn't deserve or want anymore.

"Shut it," I snapped too fast. Great, I'd probably tipped him off and made him think there was more to it. "Put your tooth in and get a damn haircut and maybe you'd have some luck, my friend," I added, trying to distract him and check his ego a bit. "You're wifed up anyway, you've got Paige."

He'd been dating Paige since we were kids.

Max knew there was something though because he wouldn't stop studying the stands.

"Hol-eeee shiiiit," he whispered under his breath, finally realizing it and laughing out loud. "That can't be…" he looked at me in awe, waiting for confirmation.

I clenched my jaw and stared straight ahead, "It's her. I fucking know it."

"Well shit, man! What's her last name now?"

"Who fucking knows. Why do you care?" I snapped again and immediately regretted it. I chastised myself for letting it come out too gruffly, I usually excelled at hiding my emotions, but seeing her leveled me down to my teenage self. I spit a curse out.

"Oooh, sensitive," he joked and shoved me in the gut. "I know she got married a while back though. Paige heard through some other girls from high school." He watched me carefully like he was waiting for a reaction. Asshole. "Paige cried for days that she wasn't invited," he tested.

"Well. It's Jules," I closed my eyes and exhaled a shaky breath. Just knowing she was sitting up there made me feel like I was shrinking. "Fuck."

3 JULES-PRESENT

I made my way up the metal bleachers, shoving my hands further in the pockets of my Louis Vuitton wrap coat- a present from my now ex-husband. I should use the word "present" lightly anyway, since I had known it was more for appearances than a true gift for me. I had to chuckle wryly to myself. I would have never worn a jacket like this before him, and as soon as it was worn out, I'd never wear one like it again. Before him I wouldn't have really thought or cared about labels. Yeah, they were nice to wear because they were usually of better quality, but it wasn't a priority. It was 100% a priority to him though and it was definitely a priority to my grandparents. Even our son, Canyon, had to be dressed to the nines every time they came around, which- I thanked the heavens- was a rare occasion each year.

I rolled my eyes thinking of the constant passive argument in our house, well, now just my house, I guess. I'd always try to convey, time after time, about how it would create bad spending habits for him to be dressing in crazy expensive labels all the time when who knew if he'd be able to keep up that kind of lifestyle as he grew into adulthood? And it shouldn't be expected of him. Canyon was a caring and sensitive little boy. Not that he would see that. But what if Canyon wanted to become a teacher like I had. I quit the pursuit when Canyon came along so I could focus my energy on him. It was always the plan to be able to go back to teaching… but it was always the plan to have more children as well… and nothing ever seemed to go my way for years. Through the entire marriage I had become an isolated glacier, melting away where no one could see.

I made my way to the top of the bleachers, where Canyon knew I'd be watching, and took a seat, scrunching my shoulders up to brace the cold. I took a deep breath and tried to relax and tell myself that no one was watching me and there was no need to feel self-conscious here. It was my place after all. I was back in the rink where I'd always been my true self, where I could always think clearer. Maybe it was the cold that made my brain shut all the distractions out and just let me enjoy. I was glad to finally share this place with my little love. And just maybe...I could get back to being myself again and embrace some real happiness for Canyon and I.

I caught Canyon's eye for a second as he filed along the boards getting ready to take the ice. He gave me a tiny smile and lifted a glove really quick before turning his attention back to his little hockey helmet-headed buddies.

I hoped beyond hope that he'd make the team and his little heart would be spared from the crush of being cut. I didn't want to have to face that trial just yet. He believed he was destined for the NHL and I wanted to keep that dream alive for him as long as possible.

"Juli-Anna!" I heard a familiar voice call out, and I scanned the parents around me until my eyes met Jen Baker's, my neighbor and mother of Canyon's buddy, Troy. I absolutely hated when people said my name in two like that. She always seemed to yell the second part too, I had no clue why.

"Did you put his name down on the registration? Because I didn't see it!" She sang as she started over to me. She had a way of talking with her entire body. I noticed she had an extra layer of makeup caked on for today's try-out. I internally rolled my eyes at her attempt to look like a twenty-year-old for the try-out.

"Does it matter?" I tried to say lightly.

"Um, yeah! I'm not saying anything but," she scanned the parents dotting the bleachers around us, "I did hear that they were trying to stack the team with…" She air quoted with her fingers: "Nice families who can afford to take their kids to the Vancouver tourney this year… and have some other fun tournaments… if you know what I mean?" She rolled her eyes and flipped her platinum hair out of her face. She scanned me up and down then, probably approving of my jacket. "You look so damn skinny! How do you do it?" She asked way too loudly, making me feel uncomfortable.

I forced a smile, "Ahh, I don't know Jen, I think I'm just small-boned. But I better go sign Canyon up then."

"Yes! Go do it now," she urged.

I stood up and walked past her. She always called attention to my looks and made me feel awkward. She was probably just insecure, but her insecurity had a way of making me feel insecure… Half the time I felt she wasn't even the same species as me- she had about a foot of height on me. Kevin always called her the Ex-Volleyballer, a nod to her tall, blonde figure. I would just internally roll my eyes every time. He had a habit of looking at other women.

She did seem to be looking out for Canyon though. Probably just because she could pawn her kid off and rely on me to take him to all the practices if they were on the same team.

I really was kind of in shock about the importance of putting his name down on the sheet though. Our kids were eight, how was money already a factor? But just because I was questioning it didn't stop me from making my way back to the lobby to make sure his name was on the right sheet. I didn't want Canyon's disappointment, or Kevin's, to be my fault.

I entered the Ice League's huge lobby, which was the warmer inside area that connected the east and west rinks, and housed picnic tables, arcade games, a concession stand, and a tiny bar. I made my way to the front where the sign-in table was located. I somehow managed to walk right past it when I entered- probably because I was feeling some second-hand nerves for Canyon.

I leaned over the wobbly portable table to scribble Canyon's name down, when I noticed a familiar name at the top of the sheet…

I immediately dropped the pen and altogether stop breathing.

I hadn't seen that name in so long. Tears stung the back of my eyes, threatening to come forward and I felt a closing sensation in my throat. Jeez, I was a 31-year-old woman. Why would seeing a name make it feel like I'd just been hit by a truck? I needed to calm my breathing down before I gave myself a panic attack.

I hadn't seen that name in so long. Not since the summer I turned 22 years old. Almost a decade ago.

Printed in all caps, I reread the name- Greyson Scott. Of course the writing looked rushed. All of his movements felt rushed and unrhythmic. The only time he smoothed out his actions was on the ice...I still had that handwriting somewhere in one of my boxes of old things... On sweet, but always slightly crude, birthday and Valentine's Day cards, signed 'Love you, Grey.' I had that last name printed on half a dozen ratty, old sweatshirts put away somewhere in my garage. I wore that last name for so many years, and for the longest time I thought it'd be mine- something that, even a decade later, made me want to break down and cry.

I took in a shaky breath. I had to hold it together. It could've been a mistake, or maybe just a nod to him- he did play here as a kid, and he did end up playing a couple seasons in the NHL. But did this indicate he was coaching this team? Last I heard he was in Michigan…why would he move back here to Minnesota? To my hometown. Sure, he'd lived here through high school, but unlike him, I was here long before and long after. I had shown him all the ins and outs of this town…. Maybe it was some kind of joke…. Or could that really be him?

I got the answer a second later.

"Ju-ju!"

I shut my eyes, wincing at my old nickname and turning my head.

"Max," I replied.

I waited a second, wondering if this would be a standoff or a nice blast from the past.

He chose the latter and walked toward me in his skates, swishing in his warm-up sweats with outstretched arms. His eyes flashed like those belonging to a little kid who had just gotten away with mischief, just like they always had. It was nice knowing that life hadn't killed that playfulness within him.

"Bring it in, Juju! Last time I saw you we were college kids drunk on the ether of youth," he laughed and leaned down to hug me. "You're still so teeny tiny!"

The hug shocked me, and it took me a second to reciprocate. Good job Jules, make him think you're a cold bitch, I thought.

"You're on skates, not fair," I said, giving him a pat on the back. Clearing my throat, I mentally tried to figure out how to ask what I really wanted to know.

"How are you? You're coaching now?" I asked, trying to gauge his involvement with this team.

"I'm better now that you're here," he winked at me and tugged at the front of my hat, but his face turned more serious. "I'm in charge of a lot of the Ice League now. I was split between the rink in Brookdale and here for the last couple years. But now they've given me the run of it. Can you believe that? I've got an eye for talent!" he laughed. "Must be because I watched more than played during my time in the net with our winning team growing up, ya know? I'm managing all of the youth Griffin teams."

While I'd practically grown up here skating, I had to remind myself that so had Max. And Grey. This place held so many memories for me… for us.

"You've got the personality for a coach," I smiled at him. He really did, he was always pretty genuinely happy. I think I'd only seen him lose it one time when his girlfriend Paige threatened to leave him. And him losing it wasn't violent, he sobbed like a baby- an aspect I had learned to appreciate in a man. But again, that was nearly nine years ago. It was amazing how he looked almost the exact same, hat still turned back, but just a few more wrinkles around the eyes, and a little more scruff.

He paused for a second and he eyed me with a suspicious smile, "You're probably wondering about who's coaching the '07's though, aren't you?"

I shrugged my shoulders and tried to fight the blush creeping into my face, "Uh… I-"

"It's Grey's team, and Smitty is assisting. In all honesty, Smitty and Ashlie- they're married-" he said with an eye-roll, "and Paige- we're not married- but they're all going to be really happy to see you. Paige is probably going to go nuts over this-"

He must have noticed my panicked face.

"In a good way of course! We had some fun times, Ju-ju! Then we just didn't hear from you. Cold turkey, Ju-ju." He shook his head. "You broke our hearts, girl! We grew up together, you were part of the gang!"

I cleared my voice and prepared myself not to choke on his name, "But this is Grey's team?" I asked, slightly shaking and hoping to break away from talking of our past.

He paused, "Yes. but don't worry about that. It'll be fine. I honestly want your little rugrat to play for my organization. He'll probably be an awesome skater…" he eyed the names on the clipboard he snatched from the table and spoke to me as he studied them, "Assuming you taught him? What's his name?"

That surprised me. I always did like Max though; we had a few heart-to-hearts back in the day.

"His name's Canyon," I smiled. It was easy to talk about my

wonderful little boy. "I did teach him. He was a natural though."

"Bowlegged like his Mommy?" Max laughed and I just nodded. It was a bit advantageous to be built that way when learning to skate, because you were already starting out with some natural edges. "Alright… kid's gotta cool name… last name?" he asked, and I could tell he was trying to catch a glimpse of my left hand. I was thankful I'd stuck it back in my pocket. For some reason, I didn't want him to know of my divorce.

"Tate," I said.

He gave a soft smile, "Well, it's nothing like Hurley, and I'm not gonna lie, I might accidentally call him Lil Hurls, but-"

"Wait," I said, "no favors though, okay? If he makes the team-great, he does want to be with his friends that are already on this team, but if he doesn't, it's probably for the best… I don't know if…"

"Damnit Ju'j," he said it jokingly, exactly how he used to say it, putting me at ease. "You worry too much. I won't let anyone know his name."

He studied me then, narrowing his eyes to meet mine, making me feel uncomfortable.

"Tate…" he said again, tsking. "Always thought you'd be a Scott girl," he drawled slowly with a sad smile.

I felt my chest tighten and my throat hurt with clogged emotion, but I tried to play off the comment with a polite smile.

With that, he gave me a wink and turned to march back to the ice.

4 GREY- PRESENT

"Did you find out the kid's last name?" I asked Max.

He pretended not to hear me while he demonstrated some goalie trick for the kid in front of him.

"Max. Did you. Find. Out?" I was grinding my teeth so hard my jaw was throbbing.

He blew the whistle and turned to me, waiting for the kids to file in front of him.

"Which kid?" He asked, clearly playing dumb.

"Don't play fucking mind games with me Max, you know who I'm talking about."

"No, I do not. Get your head in this- in what's front of you, dude," he urged me. "And no f-bombs around the kids."

I rolled my eyes, "They'll hear it in the locker room eventually. There isn't a Hurley on the list."

"She didn't have a baby all by herself, man. Would you have a kid with a great woman and not claim it?" Max said it without making eye contact, like he knew he was testing me.

He could've just sliced a knife right into my heart instead of saying that and he knew it.

Fuck. This. He convinced me to coach- no, begged me to move back here and help him out. I could've gone anywhere, but I chose to shove my past of this place aside and be a good friend. And now this shit? I had no idea which was her kid, and I couldn't go around looking into their helmets for resemblance...the tyke could easily look like the dad anyway...which would be a shame… No. Fuck. The frustration I was feeling was off the fucking charts. I could not handle seeing her on a weekly basis. The thought of that made me want to yak. I shut that particular door years ago, and it needed to stay shut…

5 JULES- 9 YEARS AGO

I was anxiously waiting in the dark parking lot staring at the rink doors, willing them to open with my eyes. I hugged myself in my long down coat, trying not to freeze in the late February night. I felt kind of awkward standing around the rest of the families and girlfriends of the players, not knowing who to socialize with. Grey's team just finished up their game and it was tradition to wait for them afterwards. They would come out freshly showered with their suits back on and chat for a couple of minutes before having to get on the team bus that drove them back to the university.

I actually found him hotter after the game than before it. Just thinking of him walking out made me feel giddy like some kind of groupie seeing their rockstar crush. He always came out all tousled and his suit- sans tie- was always crumpled and never on straight. That boy lost so many ties at different rinks around the country that I told him he should start signing them so people could return them to him.

I usually didn't make the trek to away games, but I think Grey really wanted me to be here this time. He was getting to the end of his college game days and I knew this made him nervous. I was happy to play the supporting girlfriend though. Being from Vancouver, and over 24 hours away, his parents rarely made it to games, and never away games. It'd been like that since we started dating. He'd lived with a billet families since he was 15.

Guys started walking out the heavy rink doors, and I stood on my tiptoes in my sorel boots to try to catch a glimpse of him. I was so incredibly attracted to him that I still couldn't believe how lucky I'd gotten… to have someone I loved as much as him and he loved me back too? And to get it right the very first time? I would never get tired of being with Grey, I just hoped he felt just as strongly about me. And I was hoping we'd be done with long distance sometime soon. It was easier back in high school and we didn't take advantage of it. I had to laugh at that. We could've been intimate with each other for years before we were but Grey never pushed me, he let me be my innocent high school self. I loved the guy for it.

"You see him?" A gravelly voice from behind me asked, making me whirl around and lose my balance.

"Easy babe," Grey chuckled and wrapped an arm around my waist and pulled me into him effortlessly.

My face hit his large chest and his woodsy smell enveloped me. He had a way of making me feel so wanted and secure.

He gave me a hard squeeze, "Thanks for coming, babe, means a lot."

"Anytime for my guy," I returned, looking up at him.

He bent his head down and gave me a kiss, earning him a few catcalls from some guys already seated on the bus, freshmen no doubt. I couldn't help but let out a giggle.

"You coming back to my place?" He asked with raised eyebrows.

"Want me to?"

"You don't have to ask that babe, you know the answer to that," he said pointedly.

"I know… I just like hearing you say it."

"My bed, is your bed, my tiny princess," he said, wiggling his eyebrows.

I swatted at him, but smiled. "Well then, I'll be there," I said softly, kissing his chest and looking up at him.

"Damn, babe. Now I've gotta be thinking about you in my bed for the next hour on this sausage fest bus ride. I wish I could go with you." He gave my low pony a tug and stuck out his bottom lip, making him look like a little boy mid-tantrum.

"And let the team miss their captain? No way," I reached up to touch his scruff. "Love this, by the way." The beard was a new thing he'd been trying out. The last time he'd tried to grow it he only did it because he could- not because it looked good. He had been around 18 and it was very patchy. Now it was sexy. I caught myself staring at him a couple times lately, wondering how the 16-year-old boy I fell in love with had become so manly.

"Love you," He kissed the top of my head and gave me one last squeeze. "Missed you this week."

"Love you too, and missed you just like you missed that last shot."

"Yeah, yeah," he smirked. "I'll see ya soon… and I won't miss," he gave me a slight spank and I like out an exaggerated gasp.

"So confident there, aren't ya bud!" I whispered up to him.

He backed away like he'd been shot, "My girl! Calling me bud?"

I reached his hand and pulled him back to me and made him hug me again. I loved when he called me his girl.

"I do gotta go Jules, but I cannot wait to hold you tonight," he whispered down to me.

I felt myself blush as I looked up at his dark brown eyes. With that, he headed towards the bus.

I started walking towards my car but spun around to him.

"Wait! Put your hat on before you catch a cold!" I quickly called to him, which earned a couple hoots from the bus. I grimaced and felt my cheeks heat up, feeling a little bad that I probably embarrassed him, but it was true! It was freezing out and he just showered.

But Grey showed no signs of embarrassment, he just gave me a wink as he pulled his beanie from his coat pocket and over top his damp hair.

I took that as my que to find my car and head to Brecklin.

As I started towards the parking lot, I felt a buzz in my down jacket and fumbled to unzip my phone.

Grey texted: I love being loved by you, baby.

A giddy bubble of happiness rose in my chest, the kind of feeling only Grey could give me. The kind of feeling I hoped would never end.

Grey lived alone in a brick townhouse-type of apartment next to train tracks that ran through the edge of campus. The outside reminded me of project housing. Inside it was minimally decorated, but so Grey. He'd hung a couple of Canadian and hockey flags up around the living room, but not much else. I preferred his place over his friends- who had a bunch of posters of sports illustrated models in half dress lining their walls. One of the player's girlfriends even helped purchase some of the model shots, which to me was absolutely insane. Grey laughed at my horrified face when he told me about that. "You're not gonna buy me porno pics?" He joked. I shot him a look that said 'no f'ing way.' That was not my style, and Grey knew that. "Only got eyes for you, babe," he'd say, and I knew he meant it.

Grey's place had a tiny living room with a lopsided couch, connected to a kitchenette where he made us Grey Gourmet Grilled Cheeses, as he deemed them. Upstairs were two rooms- one empty, where he ended up keeping his hockey bag and some weights, and a cot for when friends came to visit. The other room was his. His queen size bed with a plain royal blue comforter took up most of his room. He'd recently added a side table that he proudly made, which had a bible laying on it and a framed picture of us from high school. The last piece of his room was a desk- littered with notebooks and papers from class and barely ever touched.

He had zero organizational skills when it came to classes. School was not his thing- it never had been. I'd practically dragged him through his junior and senior years of high school. He'd told me a million times that school was just a means to an end for him- and his end was to play hockey. The other thing he hated about school, and I knew this was true about him, was that he hated people telling him what to do. In high school, when a teacher said to read a certain chapter, he always had the urge to say- you can't tell me what to do! His aversion for school was fine by me. I just loved him. I didn't care what he did- my grandparents did though. So, I tried hard to help him with school and help him from some kind of "back-up plan," as my grandparents called it, just in case hockey didn't work out.

"How's he going to support you?" My grandparents would ask all the time. They didn't hide the fact that they didn't approve of our relationship. Every time I stepped out of line or didn't act in accordance to their definition of the perfect granddaughter it was always Grey's fault, even if he had absolutely nothing to do with it.

I had a hunch that their dislike of him probably had something to do with hockey and my father, but every time I pushed for more information I was cut off and rudely shut up, so I eventually learned to stop trying. It sucked, but whatever, Grey was my person and had been since sixteen. I knew he would be my forever with a calm confidence I couldn't even explain.

I made the drive all the way up to Brecklin University- about an hour and a half for me- almost every other weekend- pretty much every time the hockey team had a home game or game close enough to drive to. I loved this drive. It was so much better than the long hours that used to be between us when I was at college the last three and a half years. I had wished to go someplace closer, but my grandparents financed it and their only condition was that I attended their alma mater. I did so grudgingly but finished school a semester early. I had recently moved back home and was just coaching skating. I went to school for education and hoped to be an elementary school teacher… but I'd have to wait until the spring for interviews for the next school year. That was alright with me though because it gave me a little break and I loved being able to see Grey more often- wasn't as often as when we were kids, attending the same high school and training at the same rink- but for the time being, Brecklin felt like our little oasis.

Pulling off the highway, my music was interrupted by a text. Looking down I noticed it was Grey.

Hope you're already in my bed when I walk in the door…

I caught myself smiling reading it and I quickly typed back, *How about I stop by the store and grab us some wine first?*

I slowed my driving, stalling for a bit, wondering if I should continue to his place or turn towards the grocery store, but it didn't take long for him to respond.

You take me for a rookie, Jules? That hurts. Already bought and ready for you… so bed, yeah?

I laughed out loud to myself in the car and quickly typed back I'd see him there.

6 GREY- 9 YEARS AGO

Everyone on the bus was ready to get back to Brecklin to party-ride out the high of winning with tequila and dancing… but I was ready for a different kind of high. Jules was waiting on me. Why would I go to a sweaty club to get stupid drunk and meet girls when I had the perfect girl of my dreams already: Smoking hot, absolutely drop dead gorgeous, passionate, kind, hardworking, my everything. The last few years when we'd been more long distance I'd done the party scene because Jules urged me not to miss out on it, but I would have much rather been with her. I'd be graduating this year and hopefully playing somewhere in the AHL or better and I wanted to take her with me. I'd put a ring on her first, she deserved that. If her grandparents objected, I'd steal her away and we'd elope. She'd choose me… I was sure of it. I'd choose her every time if the tables were turned.

Thinking of her laying in my bed, all tangled in my covers with her brown hair fanned out made me rock solid. I had to stop thinking about her at least until we made it off the bus. Max and Smitty were sitting next to me and they'd never let me forget it if I had a hard on while sitting on the bus surrounded by a bunch of dudes.

I planned ahead a bit tonight. Bought some Cliff's pizza, our favorite, and a bottle of Moscato for her and some red wine for myself.

When the bus came to a stop, I fumbled out as quickly as I could. I think I was the first to grab my bag from the bus and tear out of the parking lot.

I could hear the guys teasing me as I walked away.

"Somebody's wifed up tonight!" Smitty yelled.

"Tell Juju hello!" Max chided in the background.

I smiled to myself. Fuck yeah, I'm wifed up. I'd been wifed up for a while. And they were all jealous.

"Babe! I'm home!" I smiled just calling this out. I loved having her here. I looked forward to her presence all week. She was starting to make Sunday nights pretty damn hard for me. All of a sudden, my bed would feel so empty without her.

We'd never had the luxury of consistent sleepovers. We never dared to in high school- we made it out of that town as virgins, and that was totally okay with me. College was trickier, I was traveling with the team all the time and couldn't really afford to visit her in my off times. She could afford it but her family wouldn't finance it- pretty sure her granddad still couldn't stand my guts even though I'd stood by his granddaughter's side for years now. We'd had the summers together, but this semester was pretty close to my dream come true. I climbed the stairs up to my room and opened the door.

There she was, already in one of my t-shirts, hair in a messy bun- I'd for sure be taking that down- and she was blushing behind a glass of white wine.

"Fuck, babe," I couldn't keep a growl out of my voice, "so fucking sexy."

She giggled and set her glass down, as I bent down to lay on top of her.

7 JULES- PRESENT

I stared at the droplets of water running down my glass of Moscato. I couldn't walk back in that rink… and I couldn't just leave my child here. I did actually think about calling Kevin to come watch Canyon and take my place, but I was done looking to him for help. He'd just end up using the situation against me… and I knew in the back of my mind he wouldn't let Canyon play on this team under any circumstances if he knew that Greyson Scott was the coach. He'd 100 percent remember that name. Actually, calling Kevin here would probably end the tryout and bring hell down on me.

So, I was in the rink's bar. At 1 pm. During my son's tryout. Jeez, what was wrong with me? Where had my confidence gone?

The bar here had been renamed plenty of times over the years, but the current owners must've been around when I was growing up because they gave it back its original name of Benny's Box.

I always loved Benny's, it had a small town, cozy feel to it. Coming back to it after all these years, it still felt and looked the same- with signed hockey pictures and jerseys plastered all over the brick walls and Christmas lights hung up in disarray all year round. The new owners seemed to keep tradition as well with the signatures of patrons- it was tradition to sign the bar- in any place, anywhere. The bar counter and walls probably donned the youth signatures of hundreds of NHL-ers who'd stopped through here at some point in their careers.

I put my head down and massaged my temples with my fingertips.

"Doin' alright, hun?" The bartender asked in a tone that was way too peppy for my current mood. I wanted the dull waiter who served me my wine to come back.

I mumbled a reply to her, but when she didn't leave, I looked up.

Jesus. Today was apparently the day for fricken reunions.

"Paige?"

She looked at me excitedly, waiting for me to speak more.

I stared at her dumbfounded. I hadn't seen her in nearly a decade either. She looked more or less the same, with maybe ten more pounds on her, but her bleached, long blonde hair was still styled the same way, curled and running past her boobs, and she still wore too much eye makeup. She sported an antique Benny's Box t-shirt.

"Hey, girly!" She bounced up like an excited little kid. "Max texted me you were here! I am so excited to see you! How are you?!"

I still stared at her in complete shock. How was it that time had kept going by, but it felt like nothing changed when I saw her?

"What are you doing here?"

"My lover," she rolled her eyes, "and I own this bar!"

"You and Max?" I asked.

"Yes, girly!" She gave a wide grin, "We put it back to its former glory, just like when we were kids! You like?!"

I gave her a confused look, "I- I thought…" I cleared my throat. She was being so nice to me. "I figured you wouldn't like me?"

"And why the hell not?!" She rolled her eyes. "A lot went wrong and we never got your side of the story."

I felt my mouth open, but I couldn't seem to find the right words to begin.

"We never got Grey's side either though," she added quietly. "He just shut down completely after you were gone. We had no idea what happened." She gave me an expectant look, like she wanted my story. I couldn't tell her though. Not here, not right now. If I told her, she'd tell Max, and then Grey would hear my words… I was not ready for that. No way was I ready. Maybe I'd never be?

I couldn't help but replay her words though… Grey had shut down? Why? He was the one who chose to leave me and shoot into stardom on his own. I had to push thoughts of him from my head.

Instead, I offered her the obvious, "I have a son."

She clasped her hands together and bounced again, "I'm an Aunty!"

I couldn't help but laugh, only Paige would be this excited over my son and would overlook almost a decade of complete silence on my end. Tears threatened to come to my eyes for the second time today. I didn't really have any friends. I hadn't really trusted anyone since I had Canyon. It was always me and Canyon against everyone… Kevin was in our lives, but more often than not, we were in a silent agreement against him too. Paige had been dating Max since high school, so she'd known Grey and I for that long as well. She was probably still Grey's friend… but she'd been mine for a time too. A really good one.

"Do you want to see a picture?" I asked hesitantly, fumbling with my phone to pick out a cute shot of him.

I showed her his freckled missing-tooth cuteness.

"Oh my God, he looks just like you Jules," she said while studying the picture. "Even down to those little freckles! And those baby blues! Your boy's gonna be a heart-breaker, I can just tell."

"He is a cutie, isn't he? He's actually out on the ice right now." I thought about saying I'd introduce him to her… but I was still a bit unsure of this situation.

"Max said he's a little super-star out there," she winked at me. "Got the inside scoop from my boy already."

"You and Max, still going strong?"

"I mean, you could say that I guess. I think we're one of those couples that will never get married. We're trying to start a family, but we've been having trouble."

I was surprised with how open she was with me, then again, she was always an open book, unlike myself. I remember always admiring her for her ability to be like that.

"I'm sorry," I told her.

"I don't want to focus on the sad stuff though, I want to hear about you! You a high-end mama driving around a Range Rover these days or what?" She asked. I couldn't help but laugh that she'd remember what we joked about so long ago- that we'd be cool lulu wearing, mimosa sipping, Range Rover driving moms of little athletes together.

I hesitated, I wasn't sure if I should play it off and pretend everything was perfect or if I should actually let her know just how glamorous my divorced ass was becoming. She'd been so real with me…

"Range Rover- yes… but only because I got it in the divorce settlement," I said softly, looking down at my glass in front of me.

"So recently single." I couldn't help but feel a certain amount of shame saying this. I wasn't shameful that things ended with Kevin. No, that thought brought me great joy. What shamed me was the fact that my baby didn't have a good father figure because I knew deep down, I had married the wrong person. Neither of us married for love. And through our marriage Kevin had always been hyper critical and horrible to me. I drew the line when it came to treating Canyon with that cruelty. No one could talk to my boy that way. I honestly think he left because he became sick of being around me. And that was the perfect ending.

I looked back frequently wondering why I stayed with him through that hell, but I didn't really have a choice. I had to forgive myself for being young and naïve at the time.

I looked up at Paige to find her staring down at me with her mouth in a perfect o.

"Well," she said slowly. "Maybe your ex just wasn't the one?"

A picture of Grey came to mind when she said 'the one.' As per usual. It happened every time and it never hurt any less. I took in a breath and snorted, "Kevin definitely wasn't, I knew that at the start. I shouldn't have ever married him. It was kind of forced on me and at the time I was practically a space cadet. I kind of blacked out of life," I snorted.

That was the first time I'd said that out loud. I kind of shocked myself with my candid honesty. Maybe I finally needed to speak the truth.

But when Paige looked at me with sympathy, I hated it. I shouldn't have let the truth slip out. She nodded slowly, "Things happen for a reason, I guess."

They did. That was something I wholeheartedly agreed with. Because without Kevin there would be no Canyon, and my little troublemaker completed my world.

"So, are you hard-core single or dating these days?" She asked with a mischievous smile, trying to lighten the mood.

I mulled it over. I hadn't put too much thought into that question yet.

"Honestly, I want to be single, but then again, it can get lonely and I do get jealous when I see Kevin with his leggy bimbo… but not over him," I added quickly. "Just over being with someone, ya know? But I don't feel like I could trust anyone new anymore anyway."

She gasped. "The ex cheated on you?"

I just nodded. I didn't care anymore. I was actually happy 'the other woman' came around and convinced him to divorce me. It had been my only way out.

"What if it was someone you already trusted?" She questioned.

I gave her a shrug, not wanting to think about it too much, "It's all good. It just sucks because I really wanted Canyon to have siblings."

"Well, it's definitely not too late! You had an early start! Look at me and Max, we're just now trying to get started. You're only what, like 29? 30? I would just… keep an open mind," she finished, but looked like she wanted to say more. I remembered that look from our twenties and it made me smile knowing that I could still read her.

"What is it?" I asked.

"How long… um…" she looked down at the bar in her struggle for words.

"Just ask," I urged. I had a feeling I knew what her question was going to be.

"I was trying to do the math, and in no way be like mean, but just… how long after Grey was your son born?"

I knew she didn't mean to be offensive or accusing in any way. I'd been gone for a long time, but I knew deep down Paige wouldn't ever want to hurt me. On top of being so nice she'd always been an on-the-girl's-side kinda girl.

"It's ok," I played with the condensation on my wine glass again. "I've actually never talked with anyone about this past… He was conceived at the end of that summer." I looked back up at her and took a deep breath, "It was an accident, if that's what you wanted to know. And not with Grey," I said weakly, internally wishing it was a lie.

8 GREY- PRESENT

I looked at the paper with the finalized list of kids on my team. Analyzing it for I don't even know what- it's not like I could look at a bunch of random names and be able to tell what Jules named her stupid kid.

Whatever. It was all up to fate at this point. It was probably easier that I didn't know her kid's name anyway… because if I did know it, would I really be able to cut her kid? As much as I said I'd easily do it… I wasn't so sure.

"Alright, here it is. See if you agree," I sighed and handed the paper to Max.

He quickly scanned over my thoughts and nodded, "I'm with you on all this."

Still in his skates, he turned and exited his office to post the results up on the board in the lobby.

I slumped in the fold up chair in the corner of his office, he really needed to upgrade this place.

I pulled my hat off and ran my hands through my hat hair, letting out a frustrated growl. What a fucking day.

I didn't want to exit the rink for a while. Not until I was sure everyone else had left. I didn't want to face Her; it'd be too much. I wouldn't even know what to say. I don't think I'd be able to say anything at all actually. The amount of history between us in this very rink and her standing there with a different guy's ring on her finger... with a kid. Just reminding me of everything that I didn't have…and how she moved the fuck on real quick, but I was still in the same place she left me almost a decade ago.

I needed to get back to my place and have a personal day.

Max swished his way back in. He swished his way everywhere. I don't think I'd seen him wear anything besides sweats since a college jorts tailgate.

"Wanna come over for some beers?" I asked him. I honestly didn't want to be alone after today and I didn't want the company of any women either.

He shrugged his shoulders and gave me an understanding look, "Wouldn't say no to that, bud. Paige can handle the place for the rest of the day anyway. I'll tell Smitty to come too."

9 JULES - PRESENT

I found Jen mingling in the lobby of the rink.

"There you are! You disappeared! I'm thinking they'll post the finalized list soon," she said. She whispered to me then and gave a thumbs up, "Our kids did awesome."

I smiled and felt a little more at ease then. I was afraid my absence from the stands would freak Canyon out.

Right then, our little minions came bounding out rolling their hockey bags behind them.

Canyon's hair was spiked up with sweat and he was giving me a big smile.

I hugged him when he came close to me. "Great job, buddy. I'm so proud of you."

"You don't even know if I made the team, Mom," he said.

I messed with his sweaty sandy blonde hair, "Doesn't even matter. You're a superstar and we're getting froyo after this anyway," I told him.

He gave me his little sweet smirk. His friends ran past behind him and beckoned for him to go. He looked at me in silent question. He was such a good boy.

"Go ahead, I'll be here."

Right then, I noticed Max walking across the lobby to the bulletin board with a paper in his hand. I saw him scanning the parents as he walked until his eyes landed on me and he gave me a wink.

Canyon made the team.

"Girl! Did Max just give you a wink?" Jen asked me, sounding like a high school girl.

"Yeah, we actually grew up together," I explained to her.

"What?! Why wouldn't you have said something?"

Because I had no idea the three of them were back. Because I wouldn't have come today if I had known. And because I was afraid of talking about my past with their head coach, I thought.

I'd already spoken too many truths today, so I just gave her a small smile and a shrug.

10 GREY- PRESENT

We were baking in the late August sun, sitting poolside in my backyard. A few seasons in the NHL paid well. I'd jumped around to four different teams, so I never really settled anywhere for too long. Most of my life had been like that actually- moving from town to town for different teams. The longest I'd stayed in one place was when I was in high school playing for the Griffins and then college playing up at Brecklin.

After my team didn't make the playoffs last spring, I knew I wouldn't be playing another season in the NHL. I'd had one too many concussions and not enough goals, and no one wanted me. That was alright though, I achieved that dream. I just didn't know what was next and I didn't know where was next.

After being dismissed I shut myself up in my apartment in New York and drank about a week away in my boxers by myself just binge-watching random ass tv shows and people watching from my penthouse. I had no idea what I was supposed to be doing. Usually when all the guys went home during the off-season, I just stayed and trained right through it. But I had no point to train anymore, and no home to go to. My parents were still in Vancouver, but I hadn't lived with them since I was probably 14 or 15 and I didn't even consider that home. If I really thought about it, the most secure and at home I'd ever felt had been my high school years that

I'd spent in Minnesota and at the Ice League clowning around with Max and Smitty… and falling in love for my first and only time… with Jules.

At some point in that lost boxer week, I figured people went to work, but what was I even qualified to do? If I was being honest with myself- I barely did college. I had a general business degree but I knew nothing except the ice.

It was Max who swooped in and saved my ass. He had moved back to Northfield about a year after college. After a failed stint with an AHL team and then being demoted to an ECHL team for a season, he retired and started working at a couple different rinks before finding his way back to the Ice League with the Griffins. When he saw I wasn't re-signed and was probably retiring, he reached out. Thank God for that because who knew where I'd be if he didn't call.

I'd like to say that I could've gone anywhere and done anything, but that wasn't true. I was pretty lost.

I figured I'd saved most of my money and it was invested here and there, but I was due for one big purchase and that had been this house. It wasn't huge by any means, but it was sizeable and on a nice street on the wealthier side of town. It was on one of the streets I used to drive down as a teen and dream about living in one day with a family of my own. The kind of streets that were lined with uniform trees that the town decorated at Christmas time and with sidewalks that were kept up through every season. It was just too bad that the second part- a family of my own- wasn't in the cards for me. But whatever, at least I made it to this side of the town rather than crashing at a billet family's or Max's parent's place like I used to.

"Dude, you need new pool chairs, these are stiff as fuck," Smitty complained. "And you need sunscreen for pool days, man. You get a big fat zero in hospitality." Smitty shook his head.

"Well, I'm not shopping. Drink more and you'll feel less stiff," I snapped back.

"What's up his ass?" Smitty asked.

Max sighed, "wouldn't you like to know, Mr. No Show at tryouts."

Smitty rolled his eyes, "I told you I'd coach, but I wouldn't be a part of tryouts. Gives me PTSD." He shivered.

"Oh, bullshit, dude. I thought you'd know it was important for me to show a strong coaching team from the start," Max said, giving him a serious look.

"You two sound like damn girls arguing." I got up to grab another beer from the cooler.

"Isn't that his like tenth?" Smitty asked with raised brows.

"You a girl? Why are you counting my beers?" I muttered back.

"He's on the team," Max said then, cutting through everything else.

I froze. "Who is?"

He looked at me with a solid face, giving nothing away. "Canyon Tate."

I was having a hard time breathing, I knew what he was saying. I was thankful I had shades on to shield my eyes from them. "That name supposed to mean something to me?" I tried to hold an even and careless tone, but I knew Max could see right through me, he was basically my brother.

"Am I missing something here?" Smitty asked. I felt like punching him in the face. I didn't want to hear the explanation. Saying it aloud, hearing it... would make it all true... that she'd had a son without me and I'd have to face him on a consistent basis.

"Yeah. He's Julianna Hurley's son."

Hearing it felt like the floor had been ripped away from me.

"No way!" Smitty said in awe. "I thought she was gone for good!"

I felt myself put my beer down, march back into my house and make it to the bathroom before I lost my shit. The thought of talking to her again. Her. Jules. Actually face to face, made me so upset and nervous I puked up my beer like some kind of sorority girl.

11 GREY- 14 YEARS AGO

I was going to surprise her, but I heard something...

It was my girlfriend's birthday today. She was turning seventeen. That meant we'd been dating for a full year. We were the couple everyone wanted to be. She sat in the stands and cheered me on every game and I cheered her on at her competitions. We even supported each other and pushed each other during our training. Thank God I made the Griffins again this year. I knew if I didn't make the team it would mean I'd have to go back home to Vancouver. No way did I want that. I needed to stay on the Griffins and with the same billet family in order to stay near Jules. My billet family knew Jules and probably knew that I snuck out to see her, but it didn't seem like they cared. Her family lived here and she'd been training out of the Ice League since she was five. She would be riding out her figure skating career here. So, here's where I would stay. So actually, she made me better.

But that sound… almost like… barfing. Why would Jules be barfing? She didn't seem sick… she wasn't pregnant, she was a virgin. I mean- I'd know. I was the one trying to get in her pants- or like- trying not to get in her pants. Because I wanted to. But I didn't want to unless she wanted me too… but why else did people barf? I didn't want to answer that because I knew why other figure skaters barfed and that scared the shit out of me… but I couldn't see her doing that.

"Babe," I whisper yelled into the figure skaters' locker room.

I heard muffled crying then. Maybe practice didn't go so well today. Happens. She really wasn't a crier though.

"Jules, that you?" I wasn't exactly supposed to be in the girls' locker room. I made my way to the painted cinder block partition that housed the locker room's bathroom.

Jules was on the floor by the toilet, her legs pulled up against her chest. She still had her skates and skate guards on. She was so tiny, and her skates made her legs look even skinnier. She was supposed to be on the ice. I was going to leave flowers by her bag as a surprise for her when she got off.

My beautiful Jules. Even with eye makeup smeared and running down her face, she was the most beautiful girl. Her hair pulled up in a bun, her blue eyes shining at me through tears.

She dropped her head against her boney knees. "Grey, please go," she said weakly.

"Well, first off, Fuck that," I told her as I plopped down next to her and put the flowers I'd bought her by her side. I started rubbing her back and we sat there peacefully for a minute.

"Hey," I told her, waiting for her to look up at me.

But she wouldn't. She wasn't ready to talk, but I'd make her. I was not going to leave this topic alone. I would not turn a blind eye to this. No way in hell. She was my girl to protect.

"Jules," I said as softly as I could. "Look at me."

She turned her head so she could eye me slightly.

"What's going on?" I asked her.

"It's just stress," she sniffed. "It doesn't matter, everything's fine."

She was not fine. Her body was trembling like she'd just had a panic attack.

I knew regionals was coming up for her and that it would probably be her last year competing. I really couldn't understand where her head was at these days. Skating was important to her, but at the same time, she couldn't stand it.

She was burnt out and it'd been getting worse this past year. I could feel it weighing on her, especially lately- her usual bubbly self was waning and her smile seemed forced.

"It's not fine," I told her.

I let my head fall back against the wall but kept rubbing her back. I kind of felt like a failure of a boyfriend then. Why didn't I pry when I thought she looked weak and upset the other day?

"If going to regionals is going to make you sick, you shouldn't go," I told her firmly.

She stiffened under my hand, "Grey, you can't tell anyone."

I didn't respond right away. The sport was becoming toxic for her and I hated it. I could tell from watching her go through it that this sport was like a love-hate relationship. She was so good at it, and she loved being on the ice. Watching her was like an artist at work… but this past year was almost excruciating for her… because, while my hockey career was far from over- I could keep trying until I was almost thirty, maybe forty if I was lucky- her career was pretty much over after this year.

"What am I even doing this for?" She asked then. "I've been doing this my whole life and why? I have nothing to show for all my work. And now I'm just supposed to be done after this year? And do what? Start working in a new direction? It's a failed career, Greyson. I'm a failure and I'm 17," She let out an exasperated sigh.

I wanted to tread carefully here and not make her more upset.

"Babe. One- you're not a failure. By any means. Two- That's the problem- it was not work for you before. Now it is," I told her. Hockey wasn't ever considered work in my mind. "I'm here for you babe. But you've got to stop freaking out and go back to having fun on the ice. So what if this is your last year? Enjoy it. Enjoy being great out there and landing everything."

She stared blankly at the wall in front of her. "I don't even want to go back out there. But I have to," she said.

"You don't have to do anything. You could walk away right now. It wouldn't matter at all," I told her.

"My grandparents would hate you for saying that," she retorted.

That was true. I reached for her hand to lace our fingers together with my free hand. Her grandparents would want success from her this year. They would consider her walking away as failing, and they would definitely blame me for being a bad influence. But whatever. I was looking out for her. Not her reputation or anything dumb they cared about.

"Yeah, well…I only care about what you think of me."

I could tell she wanted to speak more but was hesitating.

"What?" I asked her.

"If I'm not a figure skater- If I never skate again- will you still like me?" Her voice cracked at the end and she wouldn't look at me. I stopped rubbing her back then.

"Are you kidding me?" I asked her. It almost made me mad that she even asked that. It meant I hadn't been making her feel secure enough in our relationship.

I reached for her face and turned it to mine so that she'd look at me.

"You've gotta promise me you'll stop freaking out. Because nothing can happen to you, I wouldn't be able to handle it. You are beautiful and perfect and mine. I don't care if you went and joined the circus. But don't do that because I want you close by," I said while tugging her closer to me.

She blew out a sigh of relief and rubbed her eyes. Looking at her mascara-stained hands she laughed.

"Your identity just gets wrapped into it. Like I am a figure skater. It's what makes me special. If I quit… I'm a quitter," she sighed. "I must look horrendous."

"You're beautiful, inside and out." I picked her up and pulled her into my lap. "And a sport does not define that, Jules, it doesn't define who you are." I understood what she was explaining. It was something a lot of athletes struggled with… like what do you do and who are you when you're done? I promised myself right then to be there for her and not let her lose herself.

I smoothed a thumb over her cheek, "And that's definitely not what makes you special."

She swallowed hard and I felt her relax into me.

"We are in the bathroom, ya know," she said quietly. She laid her head against my shoulder, and I kissed the top of her head.

"I don't care."

"I'm getting makeup on your favorite workout shirt," she said.

"Don't fucking care."

"Your friends are going to make fun of you," she sniffed.

"Let em. They're just jealous I'm wifed up," I said with a wry chuckle. I ran my hair through her ponytail like I'd done hundreds of times and it dawned on me. "Hey, Jules."

"Huh?"

"I love you."

I felt her tense in my arms and look up at me. She gently put her hand against my face, "I love you too, Greyson. So much."

A laugh bubbled up in my chest then, and her light giggle joined mine despite her glassy eyes. It was the first time we'd said it to each other. On the bathroom floor in the locker room. It didn't matter where we were, only that we were together.

12 GREY - PRESENT

"Why wouldn't you have told me before?" I snapped at Max.

"What- and have you throw up in my office?" He asked with bulging eyes. Max always did that- he enunciated things by widening his eyes all the way out and making big hand gestures. I usually found it funny, but nothing about today was funny.

I was going to see her in the stands watching me again but with her little husband sitting next to her. What the hell kind of sick joke was this? I felt like my knees were being taken out by someone. I was going to get sick again.

"I can't do it. I'm not going to coach." I turned to Smitty, "team's all yours, bud."

That had them both up in arms arguing with each other from across my new kitchen's island. My kitchen. Fuck. Why had I bought this fucking house in this fucking town. I did not keep tabs on her at all, but I did check to see if her grandparents were still in this town before purchasing here and I'd gratefully found that there weren't any Hurley's in Northfield. Great, that was just more evidence that she'd married and taken another guy's last name. I'd like to see him. Tell him how she was mine first and he'd never be able to have what she had given me first.

But no. That line of thinking- that's where I couldn't go. She was not mine. She hadn't been in a long time- she didn't want to be. She'd made that clear a long time ago.

I stared at the wall in front of me. Maybe I'd go out and find myself a bar fight. I could find some asshole who'd love to take a swing at a washed-up NHL-er. If someone knocked me hard enough, maybe I could forget about her. At least for the night. That would probably be the easiest course of action at this point. Violence on the ice had helped me live through the last decade.

I clasped my hands together and nodded. That's what I'd do. No one cared if I lost my head. I didn't have anything to lose except those damn memories.

I heard my front door open then, making me pause and the guys finally stop arguing.

"Hi guys!" Paige called out cheerily, causing me to groan. I shouldn't have given her and Max a key to my place.

"She's too peppy," Smitty said, and I couldn't help but silently agree. Now was not the time for the positivity she oozed.

Paige walked over until she was standing in front of me, paying no attention to Max or Smitty.

She jumped straight to the point, "this could be a good thing for you, Greyson."

I gave out a frustrated growl and ran my hands through my hair, I needed a haircut and I needed to get out of there. I didn't want a lecture in my own house.

"I don't need to be psychoanalyzed by Benny's bartender," I said gruffly without making eye contact with her. I regretted the words as I'd said them. Paige was not trying to be mean to me, but I needed her to leave me alone.

She looked taken aback. I pushed out of my chair and walked out of my house with my friends sitting around my kitchen.

I didn't even reach for my keys because I knew I wasn't in a good place.

I took the short walk down the street into Northfield's downtown. I'd always loved downtown.

I wandered around town until I found myself at Scores- the old barber shop I'd gone to hundreds of times as a teen. The girl working there kept asking me questions and looked nervous. She could probably tell how intoxicated I was. I didn't want to listen to her so

I told her to buzz it all and be done with it. Jules hated it buzzed. Good, I thought bitterly to myself. I shook my head to physically jar her out of it.

As weird as it sounded, a head massage was what I craved. It made me feel relaxed. Honestly, it was my only human touch I'd had in a while. Pathetic. I had zero game.

But barbershop drunk- interesting experience… I'd probably regret it. I hadn't had a buzz since college when we all decided to bleach our hair during a tournament. Mine was too dark and we had no clue what the word toner even meant, so it ended up orange. After the tournament win, I had to get rid of it all and start over in fear of looking like a clown forever. Smitty buzzed it close to the scalp to get rid of all the orange.

Jules had been so mad about it and I had laughed in her face over it because I really didn't think it was a big deal. But when she felt my head with a cute pout on her face, she made me regret it. She was the only person who had ever cared about my damn hair. She punched Smitty in the gut- her hardest- but definitely laughable- for being the one to do it. She even threatened him over it, saying if it didn't grow back the same, he'd be sorry. Thinking of how she'd been my tiny defender going up against a hulking division 1 defenseman over my hair brought a smile to my face, which I quickly wiped off.

I needed to remember she wasn't mine. I needed to push these memories, good and bad, back into the box I'd shoved them in years ago. I wondered yet again if I'd made a horrible mistake in coming back. She was someone else's defender now.

"Dude, what happened to your head?" Smitty asked me as soon as I opened my front door. He was glancing quickly back and forth from me and the new NHL game he was playing on my tv.

"Little short there bud, we are going into the fall," Max teased, but looked at me with unease.

Whatever, I didn't care. I just wanted it gone.

I eased my hat back on, wanting them to stop looking at me.

"I'm best-looking coach now," Smitty bragged and I rolled my eyes.

I thought they would've left my house, but it looked like they'd just made themselves more comfortable, having moved to the living room.

"Pizza will be here soon," Max told me. He paused the game then and looked at me. "Paige is pissed. Fix that before I take her home," he said plainly.

I knew I had to go fix things with her but being demanded like that irked me. I had to swallow my pride though. Max and Paige were the only ones looking out for me this past spring when I had no idea what to do or where to go. They were my family.

I exited my living room and made it back to the kitchen to find Paige gathering plates and cups for dinner.

"You have any pop or water in this house or just beer?" She asked in an even tone, looking into my sorry excuse for a fridge. I think I only had beer and eggs.

"I'm sorry," I forced myself to push out a rare apology.

She slowly rose to look at me and stood with her hands on her hips and pursed lips. She needed to be a mom someday, she'd already perfected the disappointed mom glare. That brought a smirk to my face.

"Something funny young man?" She asked, making me crack a smile.

"You've got the mom look down," I told her.

"I should by now. I'm basically a mom to all three of you," she shook her head and I could see a small smile pulling at her lips. "I can't stay too mad at you when you look like a poor little boy that's gotten his toy taken away." She sighed and plopped onto one of the kitchen barstool chairs. I took a seat next to her waiting for the lecture she'd surely give me.

"You haven't had closure," she began. "You've been stewing over questions for years. We have too. We all grew up together and we were all friends."

Her words made me want to throw up arms, but I knew I was overreacting. I drew a breath in, "Don't you dare compare, Paige. What if Max did that to you?" I asked quietly.

"I'm not comparing," she urged. "But this is what I'm saying- we don't even know what she did to you. And if we have questions when it comes to her, you definitely do. You're not the same person you used to be. You used to be happy-go-lucky, light-up-every-room, and love-your-life-hockey-guy. That summer you turned into an angry hockey monster- which worked for you for a while. You had a place to put your anger I suppose. But now you're kinda just an angry shell that moves through the day. And you need to fix it. You can't keep going like this… you're going to waste your life being stuck in this fog."

I knew she was right. I did have questions and if I was honest with myself, I would say I was stuck. I couldn't let anyone in because of her. I hadn't made a single new relationship in the last decade.

"If it makes you feel better, I think she's been stuck in a different kind of situation for the past nine years and she just recently got out of it."

That snapped my eyes to hers, "How would you-?"

"Greyson- I talked to her today. She's the same Jules. She just has extra barriers up now."

The doorbell rang then, ending the conversation. I was grateful for it. I had enough to think about when it came to Jules. I didn't want to hear about her happy, fluffy, perfect-picket-fence life she had built without me. But maybe Paige was saying it wasn't so perfect? But that hurt too. As bitter as I was, I still wanted her to be happy. It was so fucking confusing.

Jules had always had a way of seeming perfectly put together, but she could poker face with the best of the upper class. I used to be able to detect cracks in her facade easily. I wondered if I'd still be able to.

13 GREY- 9 YEARS AGO

"Grey, your girl has got it going on!" Jonesy slurred and looked at her lustfully.

I clenched my jaw.

"Keep looking at her and you'll be fucking sorry," I snapped, causing Smitty and Max to let out an "ooh" in the background.

Jonesy just laughed. Asshole freshman. He shouldn't even be in the bar.

I glanced at my girl with a little unease. She definitely had it going on. But she was also most definitely gone. Sloshed. Trashed.

I was sitting in the wooden booth with the guys on the second floor of The Westshore, the hole in the wall college sports bar that everyone watched games at during the day, then smushed together to dance in at night. The bar's open floor plan allowed me to watch the bar and dance floor from a bird's eye view.

Jules had gone to the bathroom a bit ago, then never made it back up here. She was pulled to the bar by some of my other teammates' girlfriends and then started dancing with them.

Just then, I caught her eye and we held gazes for a long minute. She broke first, winking at me and I forced myself to smile back at her, but I was a little nervous she was going to get me into a fight tonight if she kept dancing around like she was.

She ran her hand through her now shorter and blonder hair. It made me a little sad that she changed it because I loved her long brown hair.

I hadn't even recognized her when she walked up to me with shades on earlier this weekend. Neither had Max or Smitty because both of them hit on her. I almost punched Max in the face after she took her shades off and revealed her giggly self. She asked if I liked it and I choked out a yes. I mean, she looked hot, she always did. But I wasn't good with change.

Now she was heading toward the more elevated stage part of the club, giggling as she went… and she was dressed… not like her usual self.

She was dressed hot. Like really hot. She was showing off everything. I had to push down the urge to take my shirt off and put it on top of what she chose to wear. I didn't understand why she needed to dress that way all of a sudden. She was in a low-cut leotard that was basically all black mesh. I really hated those things. The ones that snapped under their crotch. For one, it was like one of those things a baby wore… and it made for way harder access to get under her shirt...and I didn't understand how that could be convenient for going to the bathroom.

During the pregame at my place, Smitty made a joke that she had to get naked to pee and Max had to hold me back. Why the hell was he thinking about my girl naked? No one should think that. Except me. I was probably already riled up because of their comments about her earlier.

I rubbed a hand over my eyes.

Max nudged me then and I looked up to see him sliding another beer my way, "Dude, chill. She's just having fun. If you go all control freak on her, you'll be just as bad as her grandaddy."

I clenched my jaw at that too, shoving away a mental image of him. I was nothing like him.

"He's right," Paige offered earnestly. "Just have fun with her. That's all she wants, and it shouldn't be too hard to do. Go dance with her and show everyone she's yours if you're so concerned." Paige gave me a pat on the arm and then started pushing Max out of the booth.

He took the hint and relented that he was going to be dancing tonight.

"Get your girl!" He called back at me as he was being dragged down to the first floor by Paige.

I took a swig of my beer. They were right. I needed to loosen up a bit.

I made my way down the stairs, being slapped on the back and offered knuckle punches for winning our game as I went.

Down on the first floor, I pushed myself through the initial slight claustrophobic feeling I always felt at parties and made my way through the sweaty bodies to find my girl.

Finding her, I took the drink from her hand and gave it to the girl next to her. Jules did not need anymore. She gave me a funny look then. But I grabbed her by the waist and carried her across the dance floor to where Max and Paige were dancing. I could hear her giggling softly through the thick club music blasting.

She danced around with Paige some, and then paid attention to me. She was arousing me.

"You're mine," I said, pulled her closer to me.

She giggled and turned her neck to look up at me. "That ok with you?" I felt my eyebrows pinching together. I didn't want to sound as possessive as I felt.

"Makes me feel like the luckiest girl," she said seriously with heavy lidded doe eyes.

That was enough to make me feel secure.

I leaned down and kissed her neck. I felt her knees go weak and she let out a tiny gasp. She was totally wasted and easily turned on. She probably had no clue what that gasp did to me.

The rest of the club faded away, and it felt like it was just the two of us on that floor.

I rarely woke up before her, but I loved waking up with her in my arms. Her tiny body drowning in my clothes used as Pjs. Absolutely loved it. Her face was laying on my chest and our legs were tangled together- her leg looking tiny inside the two of mine, her one arm tucked in close to my chest and the other looped around my body. Her boobs were pressed into my body and I was trying hard not to get a full-on boner while she was sleeping.

I tried to move her a bit without waking her up; she'd fallen asleep with her head on my arm and I was starting to lose feeling of it.

I felt her shiver a little and I promptly pulled the blankets up on her. I was always a furnace when I slept but I knew she was always freezing, we made a good pair like that. She always complained when I left the window open at night and she'd pull me on top of her as a blanket, I'd laugh and comply every time.

When we were young, I'd leave the window open as an excuse for her to pull me close. I'm not sure if she ever caught on to that.

I sniffed her hair. It smelled the same lavender smell I loved, it just looked so different.

Something was going on in that head of hers. I smoothed her now platinum hair that only grazed the top of her shoulders out onto the pillow. It wasn't a big deal, I loved her, not her hair, but I kind of hoped she would change it back soon. I just felt like it wasn't her.

Last night had been the craziest I'd ever seen her get. She'd 100 percent be hungover today. She'd been building up to that, drinking more than usual the past couple weekends.

Jules was usually very even-keeled and open with me. She didn't do shots or dress slutty… or end the night with drunk crying like she had been lately. Not only was it bad that she was drunk crying, but she kept telling me nothing was wrong. Like bullshit. It just wasn't her. I liked her without all that makeup, in my pjs, and when she actually communicated with me. I probably should've dug deeper last weekend so I would've had a heads up about the sudden hair change.

I went to Paige after last weekend and asked her what the hell was up with my girlfriend, but Paige scolded me about that kind of thinking and told me I was being selfish. I was afraid she was going to slap me. She told me she supposed Jules was just feeling pressure and wanted to feel "liberated." She'd just graduated and she had a semester and summer to herself before she had to get a "big girl job." This was her time to be free and not be judged by anyone, especially not me.

That made me a little nervous though. Free of what? Free of me? I couldn't lose her. That just wasn't an option.

She stirred a little then.

"How's my little booze bag doing," I asked her quietly.

She covered my mouth and gave a pained laugh with her eyes still closed.

"I'm sorry," she said, with her hand still covering my mouth.

I licked her hand and she squirmed.

"Don't be sorry, we had fun last night," I told her, wrapping her up and kissing her forehead. But I did want to ask her if everything was alright and why she felt the need to suddenly have a wild streak and be dancing with the crazy-ass girlfriends of the team. She usually stayed tucked close to me at the bar getting happy tipsy, not trashed.

"I wish I could see inside that pretty head of yours," I said looking down at her.

"It's dumb and blonde now, why would you want to do that?" She responded kind of bitterly.

"Hey, don't say that," I adjusted myself to lay on my side facing her and gave her a confused look. "Is something wrong?"

She looked beautiful as she lay there with a slight pout on her face. She put a hand up and felt my beard like she was studying it and I just waited for her to talk. We'd been dating so long now that I considered myself an expert in understanding her, but lately something was off. I found that if I gave her silence, she'd eventually fill it.

She sighed a couple of times before almost starting to speak and then she'd cut herself off, which was just worrying me even more.

"Are you upset with me?" I asked her suddenly.

"Not at all," she quickly replied, laying her hand on my chest. It felt comforting. She had no idea how tight it felt as she was sitting there sighing.

"Nothing else matters then, babe," I used my thumb to smooth the smattering of freckles under her eye. I loved when she didn't have makeup on and I could see them.

"Never shave again," She relaxed into a smile. "I love your beard."

Truth be told I was just getting a little lazier with shaving. It itched but I didn't mind her extra attraction to me. She played with it and it felt nice.

"And I love you," I told her. "But what if I bleached it blonde and cut half it off, wouldn't you wonder why?" I raised my eyebrows at her.

She sighed again and started to pull her hand away. I grabbed it back and kept it on my chest. "I'm sorry," she said, not meeting my eyes.

"No need to be sorry. I like it," I reached out and tucked stands behind her ear. "It just took me by surprise," I tried to explain. "Very edgy though," I said, trying to sound positive.

She arched an eyebrow at me, "You've never been good with change, Mr. Scott." She blew out a breath. "I regret it. I just wanted to be spontaneous and show that I can make my own decisions about myself. But now you probably don't even like me anymore," she patted my face. I would've been mad if she said that last part for real, but I knew she was joking. Our relationship was much stronger than trivial things.

"Are you petting me?" I asked her as I pulled her on top of me. "You're drop dead gorgeous, babe." I pulled her hair back and piled it messily on top of her head. Some strands fell down because they were too short. "No matter what."

She laughed and dropped her head down flat against me and we laid there in comfort for a couple minutes, silently enjoying cuddling. I could lay there like that with my arms around her all day and be a happy man. But anxiety was coming off her in waves and I knew she wasn't happy.

"Is it because your grandparents?" I asked quietly, my mind racing to put things together.

She stiffened in my arms and then I felt her nod against my chest.

I ran my hands down her back and then back up again, trying to relax her.

"What if I stayed here with you and never went back?" She mumbled against me so quietly I could barely hear her.

I honestly wouldn't mind. I knew a lot of guys who didn't want their girlfriends around all the time, but that just wasn't me, it wasn't us. But as much as I'd like her here, I knew Jules well enough to know she was too responsible for that. She wouldn't want to hide from life or hurt her grandparents like that. She felt deeply and being disconnected from her family would weigh on her. Even though they barely gave a shit and it broke her heart all the time, she continued to try with them. My heart hurt for her.

"If that's what you want, babe. But I don't know if it really is?"

I felt her slump against me. "I don't know anymore. They're not hearing me."

"Hearing you about what?"

"About everything," she sighed again and gave me a serious look. "You want me to be honest?"

I rolled her off me to look in her eyes pointedly, "Yes, Julianna Louise. Spit all of it out right now so I can actually be a good boyfriend and help the next time you drunk cry on me."

She scrunched her nose at me for calling her by her full name, "I am sorry."

"Don't be, babe. It's my job… but you're not letting me be very good at it here," I told her pointedly.

She nodded and then turned her body towards the ceiling and kept her eyes that way, away from me, as she said the rest in a rush: "They want me to go to grad school and they want me away from you."

"Away from me…?" I asked dumbly.

"They want us to break up, Grey. It's been a constant argument and I'm so so sick of it." She faced me then, almost questioning me, and I didn't like it.

"You don't want that, do you?" I forced myself to ask it slowly but I felt panicked.

"Hell no."

Jules barely ever cursed, so I knew she was saying this with conviction.

"I don't understand why they hate me so much," I looked into her eyes trying to search for the answer. I'd always wanted to ask her if it had something to do with her father. He'd been a legend hockey player. You'd think they'd want someone resembling their son to enter the family. I didn't want to push her for answers when she was already stressed, and besides, she really didn't know much about her father in the first place - it was a conversation she always pushed away. She seemingly placed the subject of her dad in a locked away place somewhere inside her head where I was not allowed. It didn't seem like a healthy coping mechanism, but what did I know? And her grandparents were worse than her about it. When I first met them, I mentioned their son and how he was an inspiration to kids like me and it was like I mentioned something horrible. Her grandfather snapped back something about being a "womanizer." I could tell from that interaction that Jules really was truthful in the way that they never ever mentioned him. I'd told her I'd be there for her if she ever did want to talk or find out any info about him- the hockey world was small, I was sure I could find some answers somewhere- but she never brought it up. I pushed the thoughts of her grandparents away and focused on my girl.

"We're gonna be together forever babe," I pet her head to try to make things lighter and to ease her worry. "You know I want that right? A backyard with a big rink that I make for our babies, all of it," I said as earnestly as I could.

She giggled in response, then covered her mouth and blushed for laughing at me.

"You think that's funny?" I tickled her side, making her squirm against me. Her side was her weakness.

"Is that what adulthood is?" She wheezed in between laughs. "Backyards and babies?"

I eased up on the tickling and let her fall limp on top of me again.

I found her lips and said, "Yes," against them.

"Our backyard. My babies inside of you." I pinched her flat tummy.

She giggled again, "Baby, you're making me horny."

"My plan is working then," I winked at her. "Grad school though?" I asked her wearily. That didn't sound like her. She loved everything about teaching. She seemed like she had so much fun during her practice placements. It was good for her. It was the first time she seemed like she had a direction and was motivated since she quit skating years ago. When she talked about teaching her face lit up. She could talk for hours with a smile on her face telling stories about what the kids said each day. But if grad school was what she wanted, I didn't want to stop her from going. I'd never stop her, even if that meant delaying the plan I had for us after I graduated.

"You want that?"

"I don't know," she said quietly. "I'm getting… confused about what to do."

I paused, studying the rays of sunlight coming in from my tiny window and trying to choose my words carefully, remembering that I didn't want to be anything like her controlling grandfather.

"You loved teaching, Jules. Plain and simple. Stick with what you love. I think you'd be making a mistake if you went in another direction. It's up to you though, babe." I wanted to be honest with her. "But can you promise me something?" I asked her, looking down at her serious face.

"Yes?"

"Can you just toe the line with your grandparents until I finish school and get my degree so I can whisk you away easily?"

"What does that even mean?" she laughed.

"Like don't do drastic shit to make them hate me," I told her. "They already want me burned at a stake."

She formed an o with her mouth then. "Yeah, that's probably for the best," she laughed. "I don't understand how they think you did my hair. You should tell them you hate it."

"Not true, babe."

"You think I can't read you, Greyson Patrick Scott?" She asked with a smirk. "You hate it."

"It's you I love, not your hair, babe."

She gasped and swatted my chest, "you do hate it!"

"False!" I told her, grabbing her little hips. "I thought you were horny; I'll help you fix that."

She collapsed in laughter against me again, and I loved it. I loved her.

14 JULES PRESENT

It was the first day of Canyon's third grade school year. It'd gotten easier each year to drop him off, but this year didn't follow suit. I packed his lunch and put a little note in it wishing him a good day, gave him a cheery smile, and hugged him tight before he ran off into line with his friends, but as soon as I got back in the car, I bawled my eyes out.

I drove the three miles home in an absolute mess and then sat in my driveway for twenty minutes looking at pictures of him that I'd taken this past summer. I was pathetic. I needed to get some friends or a job or something. Canyon was my little person and we'd grown even closer this summer now that Kevin was barely in the picture.

Kevin showed up every other weekend and took him out for ice cream or watched the games that he had that weekend, but he wasn't a supportive dad. He always criticized Canyon to me thinking that Canyon couldn't hear what he was saying. Kevin obviously didn't realize how intuitive his child was, and then he'd wonder why his "own son was giving him a cold shoulder" and if I had turned his son against him.

I stared up at my house. It was a lovely home. Not too small, not too big, all modern farmhouse looking with brick painted white and wood shutters and accents, just outside of downtown, and at the end of it a cul-de-sac. I loved it. It was my first and only big purchase after the divorce. What an absolute joke of a marriage. It was more of a financial tie than a marriage.

I had wanted to leave him long before the divorce, but I would've lost everything. And let's face it- something I realize I have to admit to someone aloud one day according to my therapist - I was scared of him. But my grandparents had made sure I'd stick it out with him regardless of my feelings and well-being, all to avoid embarrassment at the hands of their country club friends. Pathetic. I wondered how they felt about Kevin choosing to leave me. I don't think they thought about that potential scenario, I thought snidely.

After I had found out I was pregnant with Canyon, my grandfather promptly cut me off and then gifted his business to his right-hand man in the company: Kevin. Which meant they gave all their assets over to Kevin instead of having him pay them off… they had enough money to live off, and they called the business my inheritance. But that meant all my inheritance - even what my father had penned to me before his death- was tied up and gifted to this shit of a man, and I couldn't do anything about it. I'd have nothing if I left him. I'd lose the only gift my father had ever given me. But they were already embarrassed to have a knocked-up granddaughter. An unmarried one or one who left her baby daddy instead of marrying him would be an even greater disgrace in their eyes. What would they tell everyone? I was 22 and had no form of income and hadn't even started my career. Who was going to hire a first-year teacher who would only be there half the year? What could I do but stay with him? I had no choice if I wanted to protect my baby.

Turned out, Kevin leaving was the best thing that could've happened. Because of it being his choice, he had to give me half of everything in the settlement. That was plenty enough for Canyon and I to have a fresh start.

The divorce settlement this past spring was less than messy. Kevin did not even try to get custody of Canyon, which was all I would've fought him on. He did drop hints throughout that he was doing me a favor by not fighting for it and the threat that he would fight if I did anything less than acceptable as a mother in his eyes was always there.

I needed to start a life for myself though. I couldn't just hide out in my house when Canyon was gone.

I needed to do something with my time. Getting a job would be better than hanging around here. I hated how lonely and pointless I felt with Canyon gone at school.

I decided I needed a jog. It was a crappy day out- the sky was threatening to cry too, making it a drizzly mess, but running outside would be a thing of the past in a couple months when Minnesota decided to start freezing. A run would clear my head. Maybe I'd get in amazing physical condition with all my free time.

I quickly entered my house, trying to wipe away my gross mascara stains, and changed into some running clothes.

I threw my hair in a ponytail as I walked down the front porch steps, turned my music full-blast, and let my feet pound the pavement.

After running through my entire neighborhood in the drizzle, I'd decided to push myself further. I figured if I made it to downtown, I could always call myself an uber to get back home. Besides, I had nothing else better to do with the day.

I turned onto third street where I knew I could find a Starbucks, when the familiar outline of a man stopped me in my tracks.

I could tell it was him walking from behind.

He looked like a hockey player, there was no getting around that. He looked the exact same as he did nine years ago, just more filled out now, stronger. He was a towering 6'4. He'd shot up through high school, opposite of me who stayed a solid 5'2.

A thin hoody tank covered his built chest. He had his hood pulled up and was stretching his legs. He must've been on a run as well. The exposed muscles in his arms bulged. I noticed right away he had finished the sleeve of tattoos on his right arm. It made him look even more impossibly tough. The last time I'd seen him he had only one on his upper arm, a tribute to Tenny Park in Minnesota. He said that was his home. It was the place he'd grown up and loved me versus where he was born in Vancouver. Now I wondered what else filled the sleeve… and if he covered that tribute to our home.

I couldn't move. I wasn't sure where to go. Did I turn and hide? Or did I face this head on? My entire body felt hot. How did one say hello to the person they lost their virginity to? To the only person they ever loved? The person who'd been their everything for six years- longer than some marriages. I had envisioned this meeting between the two of us so many times in the first few years after it was over. Sometimes it'd be a happy reunion...sometimes I envisioned myself slapping him in his stupidly handsome face. But that dream died a while ago when I figured we'd never see each other ever again.

I needed to make a decision.

After holding my breath for what felt like a full minute, I took a step forward onto the brick sidewalk. I'd take my time walking towards Starbucks and leave it up to fate. If he turned around and saw me, it was meant to be. If not, same. In the back of my mind, I knew I'd be slightly disappointed if I didn't finally speak with him today. I needed to rip off the Bandaid. My son had spoken to him and interacted with him and I hadn't yet. That felt so odd to me. But he probably hadn't even known it was my son. Canyon had Kevin's last name.

I all of a sudden felt very conscious of what I was wearing and berated myself for not re-doing my makeup.... what did it matter though? It's not like I was trying to impress him. After playing in the NHL he probably had some model girlfriend. I just needed to break the ice. For Canyon, I told myself.

I was ten feet from Starbucks and him when he turned around.

He stared at me and took out his headphones.

Neither of us moved.

"Uh, hi," I told him.

He looked like he was afraid to speak.

"Jules?" He pulled down his hood and blinked his dark eyes several times, focusing them on me.

"Uh... yeah. Hi."

It felt like neither of us knew what to say or how to interact with one another. Did I give him a hug? Did I nod and just walk by?

He was silently studying me there on the sidewalk.

"Were you crying?" He asked quietly.

I felt sheepish then and looked away, "It's Canyon's first day back at school," I offered lamely, feeling my cheeks heat up. "I guess I'm just one of those crazy moms," I tried to joke and roll my eyes, but it came out flat.

He abruptly stepped toward me, making me flinch, before pulling me into a hug.

It felt so comforting that I nearly cried. His hug felt the exact same as it had for so many years. His chest was so broad and warm. But it didn't last. He turned rigid and awkwardly pulled back.

His quick embrace was replaced with the freezing cold. It felt like it'd gotten ten degrees colder.

"I..uh... sorry, I didn't mean to... uh," His eyes shifted beyond me.

"Thanks," I said, cutting him off and taking in a shaky breath.

He turned to walk away, but then turned back. "Where is he going to school?" His dark eyebrows pinched together in curiosity.

"Caraway Elementary," I gave a soft smile, where I had dreamed of teaching, but never got the chance to.

Words didn't have to pass between us for me to know he remembered the name. He just nodded slowly.

"Did you just move back?" I pressed. I got another slow nod in return. It looked like he was being tortured, but he wasn't leaving.

I nervously reached up to fix my hair and he watched my hand.

"Your hair… it's uh… it's long again." His voice sounded pained. "It's nice…" he cut his eyes away from mine.

I took the opportunity to study his face. He looked the same, just older, and more tired. He left scruff on his face, but it was cleaner than when he was a kid. He was sporting a buzz cut again. He'd only had that once when we were dating and I'd been mad at him about it. It was laughable now, how I'd been upset about something so childish. With age he'd grown tougher looking. He had the same gap in his left eyebrow, from stitches he had acquired during a game in college and he still had a scar on the right side of his bottom lip from where he took a stick to the face in high school when he and Smitty were goofing off. But now he also had a jagged scar, gash really, on the left side of his face, that cut under his cheek bone. It looked like whatever it was that caused it had gotten him bad, and it bothered me that I didn't know what it was from. It was just another reminder that life hadn't stopped when we ended, even though it felt like it did.

"That scar- " I started to ask but wondered if it was too personal.

"What about it?" He asked breathlessly. His dark eyes were staring at me intensely, making me feel uncomfortable.

"What's it from?"

The silence seemed to stretch for a mile between us.

"What?" His face cracked with emotion when he said it. He looked at me like I lost my mind and like he'd just been punched in the gut at the same time. I didn't understand what I'd said so wrong. I guess it was too personal and I started to apologize, but he cut me off.

"Tate?" He spat the name out angrily.

That one word felt like a brick wall being slammed between us.

"Uh-" I stammered. "We, um… divorced."

He opened his mouth like he wanted to say more, but someone chose that moment to walk out of the coffee shop door between us and distract him.

When I saw him again he looked stoic.

"I guess I'll be seeing you and Canyon at the League then."

Those who didn't know him would say he looked calm. But he still had the same tell he did as a sixteen-year-old boy. His jaw throbbed angrily as he grinded his teeth.

"Yeah, he's excited for it," I said softly.

He gave me a nod pulling up his hood and he turned on his heel to jog away, leaving me feeling even more lonely than before.

15 GREY - PRESENT

So many emotions whirled around in my head I couldn't decide what to feel. But anger won out. I honestly didn't think it could get worse. But I realized the only thing worse than her being with another guy, was her being with some guy who just threw her aside. Fucking hell. That's where that guy belonged.

That also meant she'd traded me in for someone who didn't even care about her... I was that unimportant to her? All of my memories of the League were wrapped up with memories of her. She shook my world. I was owned by her. She was a hell of an actress if she really never cared or loved me back.

And she didn't remember how the side of my face was slit open? It was that unimportant? Just a tiny blip in her timeline of events that she hadn't even felt the need to commit it to memory; yet every time I looked in the mirror, I was reminded of the night that halted my whole life.

I tried to clear my head as I ran, but every car that passed brought me back to that damn night when everything had gone so wrong.

16 GREY – 9 YEARS AGO

Max, Smitty, and I had been drinking all day, waiting for our girls to arrive. We'd been celebrating the end of college for the last week and we were going out with a bang today because it was Cinco de Mayo, and our last weekend before graduating.

It was probably not good that we had so much free time all week. Playing hockey through school we never had time to ourselves; every minute was dedicated to training or trying to pass a class, so we didn't really know how to use the free time when we had it. This week was probably extremely counterproductive because we just worked out and then trashed our bodies by partying all night.

And then there was the tattoo incident. The three of us were shit faced and bored in the middle of the day on Monday, so we decided to go for it. I'd been wanting to start a sleeve for a while and decided I needed to start right at that second. I was happy with it: a depiction of outdoor skating at Tenny Park on my right upper arm. The image was etched in with just black ink and detailed trees surrounding the swirl of the ice-covered river and small figures playing pond hockey, and a tiny figure doing a layback as well.

Sleeves looked tough as shit. and I wanted to keep Minnesota with me wherever I went. Don't get me wrong, college had been a great experience, but skating at the League with these boneheads and Jules, and pond skating every weekend of the winter out at Tenny Park had defined growing up for me. It had also been the place where I'd looked into Jule's eyes for the first time and knew that she was it for me. She was my heart and my home. And now it was on my sleeve, literally. I was a fan.

Brecklin was probably my second favorite place to play. I would miss playing for the rowdy student section and playing on the same team as my buddies, but I was so relieved to be done with school.

I honestly didn't care about having a degree, but Jules cared, so I kind of had to in extension. I wasn't going to walk in the graduation ceremony, but Jules convinced me too, telling me we'd have one last fun weekend if I stayed.

Thank the Lord college was over though and thank the Lord I had a place to play the next fall.

I signed to play with an AHL team in Texas and I was planning on asking Jules to come with me. I was keeping it a surprise that I got signed until tonight when I planned on asking her. She hadn't accepted a job just yet, and she could teach anywhere, but I knew she needed time to start applying for this fall. It'd be a perfect start to our lives together. I couldn't wait to see her face when I told her about signing and I couldn't wait to hear her say yes. I was kind of buzzing with nervous excitement because this was pretty damn close to proposing. I did think about proposing but my buds convinced me to wait and rack up some cash first so her grandfather would find me suitable. That was true, while we could elope this year, Jules could probably have the wedding of her dreams if we waited a year or two. We had time, our relationship was strong, I didn't need to rush things when it came to us.

Paige and Ashlee arrived first and cracked open some alcohol and other fruity liquids and started mixing drinks with little umbrellas in my little apartment's kitchen.

Paige handed one to Max, who was sitting back on the lopsided old couch he had purchased for my place. He and Smitty were RA's for the younger players on the team who the university made live in the dorms for their first two years. They hated it, but it was required as co-captains. They spent most of their time at my place anyway.

"Dude, you look like a chick," Smitty teased, dropping himself onto the couch, causing it to almost drop down to the floor.

"You're taking that piece of shit with you right? I don't want it," I pointed out to Max.

Max rolled his eyes, "Try it," he said handing his drink to Smitty, "I'll drink anything my girl makes, she's a beast bartender."

I stood up then, I wanted some. I needed to keep my buzz and bravery for tonight.

I heard a car park out front then.

My Jules. I smiled easy seeing her tiny body jump out of her black Jeep Cherokee. Her newly blonde hair was thrown up into a short pony on top of her head for the drive here. I still couldn't get used to her as a blonde and I kind of hoped she would change it back soon. I had to remind myself to be supportive of what she wanted too… I did start a tat sleeve without telling her, which was definitely a double standard… and maybe worse if she hated it because I did not have the desire or funds to get rid of it. Also, I'd never admit it, but it hurt like a motherfucker to get and I heard it was worse getting one removed.

I stood out on the porch waiting for her.

As soon as she made eye contact with me, my heart hitched. Our connection would never get old. That girl owned me.

Delight overtook her face and she ran up to me and jumped into my arms. I scooped up her butt and she wrapped her legs around me. She immediately found my mouth, and made out with me fiercely, her boobs pushing into me. God, I had missed her.

We'd gone three weeks without seeing each other because I'd been busy wrapping up the school year and she'd been applying and interviewing at various places around the state.

She gave one more quick kiss and pulled back from me then, "I've missed that! Let's never be apart that long again, ya?" She said as she patted my cheek.

"One hundred percent agree," I laughed. After being able to see each other so often this semester I didn't want to go back to the long distance we had through college. "Never again, baby."

She pulled back and giggled, her blue eyes sparkled happily, "are you drunk already?"

"Nope," I lied.

She turned my hat backwards and kissed me again, "You can put me down now Mr. Scott."

"Nope, gonna hold you all night. All mine," I mumbled against her lips, earning more giggles. I loved being able to hold her so easily. When we had first started dating, yeah I could carry her, but not for long. While I had filled out a ton the last four years if I say so myself, she pretty much shrank in tone, becoming even lighter if possible. Now I could probably carry her around all night long if I wanted to.

I carried her into my living room where we were greeted with cheers from the rest of the crew.

I placed her in a seat next to Paige and turned to pick up my drink when she caught sight of the ink peeking under my short sleeve.

"Greyson Patrick Scott!" She hissed.

Everyone kind of stopped and looked. My face faltered. I hoped she wouldn't be mad because I wanted today to go perfectly. I would just have to explain that it was too late now. That's what I'd told my mom, and I hoped it would work on her too.

I heard Smitty softly joke to Max, "here we go!"

She stood up, not taking her eyes off the sleeve and came close to lift it.

I consciously kind of flexed, not wanting my girl thinking I was weak.

I saw her eyes skim over it, studying it. She put a finger in the collar of my shift to pull me closer to her. That was her sign for wanting to whisper into my ear.

"That's so hot," she giggled into my ear. My dick perked up at her hot whisper, didn't take much when it came to her, and my eyebrows shot up in surprise.

The crew went about their business then. They were probably disappointed with not getting a firework reaction out of her.

"You recognize it?" I asked her.

She smiled in remembrance, and I was struck with the need to kiss her beautiful smile again, "Tenny Park. How could I forget our first date?" she asked.

"Just wait til you see the next one I have planned, baby," I whispered and wrapped my arms around her and pressed a kiss against her temple.

After spending hours hopping around to all of the Brecklin bars, we started to get our drunk asses back to my place. We shared a loud uber to Taco Bell and then feasted like kings in my tiny living room space.

Paige and Max, and Ashlie and Smitty decided to crash at my place in the living room and extra bedroom.

Poor Paige and Max were sharing the cot in my extra room, which I don't think they would've done sober.

Jules and I retired to my room then.

I closed the door softly.

"Dance with me," I whispered to her.

She giggled, "we just danced the last three hours away," she said softly back.

I grabbed her hand gently and pulled her close to me.

"No, slow dance. Here, stand on my toes." We'd done this hundreds of times as high schoolers, messing around in the Hurley's almost permanently vacant kitchen. I remember always thinking that was sad, how Jules never had anyone waiting for her at home. But she had me. Always.

Her head only made it to the middle of my chest. She wore heels so often I sometimes forgot how tiny she was.

"You're so small," I teased her.

She kissed my chest and looked up at me. Killed me when she did that. Made me feel invincible.

"Fuck, babe."

...And then we did just that.

Coming down from our high, with our limbs tangled around each other, I faced her in the dark and dared to ask what had been in the works for what felt like an eternity.

"Julianna, will you move in with me?"

She turned to me, looking so serenely beautiful.

"Yes," she smiled. "I was hoping you'd ask."

Feeling my chest swell, I grabbed the back of her neck and kissed her, "You don't even know where I'm going and you just said yes?" I asked, amazed.

"I'm going with you, wherever you go," she said confidently with a nod.

"Texas."

"Texas," she repeated and smiled. "They signed you, didn't they?" She touched my cheek, "Congratulations, baby. I'm so proud of you."

The next morning, she put on a white dress with a blue ribbon on it for my graduation, which matched my blue robe. My parents couldn't make it, but that was okay because she was my family. She was probably the one who cared the most and was the proudest of this degree anyway.

My dad found it funny that she cared so much about a piece of paper when my real accomplishment was signing with an AHL team in Texas.

She sat with Paige and Ashlie during the ceremony, Paige would be taking another year to graduate, so she wasn't up here with us. Ashlie was in cosmetology school back home in Northfield but had come up to watch Smitty walk.

Jules took about a thousand pictures of me and with me, which felt a little ridiculous, but it made her happy, so I obliged. I had missed her graduation back in December because it was a game weekend, so it was the least I could do.

After graduation, we packed my entire apartment up in a couple of hours and loaded everything into Jules's car. I was quite the minimalist besides my hockey gear, so it wasn't too big of a job. I was going back with her to Northfield to train at the Ice League all summer and staying at Max's parents' place. Max was sticking around Brecklin to coach a clinic and kindly offered his bed back home to me until I'd be moving to Texas come August.

Max's mom was the best. I was afraid I was imposing, but she called me and told me she was looking forward to having one of her "bonus sons" come back. She'd honored only me and Smitty with that title.

I could tell Jules was tired from the long day and I told her to take a nap in the passenger seat.

She nodded, sleep already coming down heavy on her eyelids.

I was driving down the interstate for about a half hour listening to some new country jam Jules had uploaded onto her playlist.

That was when it happened.

It's funny, the stupid details you remember when you come close to death. My life didn't flash before my eyes. I just remember her nodding-off head and that dumb playlist.

In the dark, I saw the brake lights of the old pickup truck in front of me swerve fast. So fast that I had no time to figure out why the hell they'd done that.

A split second later I saw the eyes.

I slammed on the breaks and tried to swerve the wheel as hard as I could.

I should've just hit the thing.

Because what you don't remember when you're trying to avoid

one deer, is that there's usually another deer coming after it.

I swerved just enough to hit the next one and the direction I'd aimed the car caused us to leave the highway.

Glass sprayed everywhere. My body hit the wheel harder than any check I'd ever felt on the ice. I felt the shift of gravity and heard the horribly loud crunching of glass and metal telling me we'd flipped.

17 JULES - PRESENT

I parked the car and Canyon and Troy immediately unbuckled and started to hop out.

Today was the first team practice, and I'd been right- Jen had already wrapped me into carpool duty. I didn't mind though- I liked watching Canyon's practices… I just wasn't so sure if I'd like them anymore considering who would be on the ice with him. But I needed to push those feelings aside. Canyon was more important. I wanted to be a present and caring parent for him, different than how my own grandparents had been with me.

"We're gonna run in, okay Mom?!" Canyon called to me.

"Go ahead, honey. Buddy system!" I called to him.

I wasn't too crazy about him going anywhere alone, but I didn't want to embarrass him either.

I gave them a head start into the rink and kept a sharp eye on them as they entered.

Other kids his age were swarming in and out of the rink.

"It's funny," the low gravelly voice coming from behind me made me jump, "hearing you called Mom."

I turned to face Grey and tried to calm my breathing.

"It suits you," He said firmly from behind his sunglasses. I couldn't read his expression, but his mouth was in a grim straight line.

He nodded his head to me, pulled his baseball hat lower and

jogged lazily into the rink, leaving me in the parking lot wishing I could've opened my mouth to say something.

After I entered the rink, I quickly chose a seat in the bleachers, covered myself with my designated blanket, and sipped my hot chocolate as I watched the practice.

I couldn't get over my son sharing the ice with the three boys I'd grown up with.

If my high school self could peak in on this scene, she'd assume Canyon was Greyson's son.

I found myself watching Greyson just as much as I was watching Canyon.

I was catching glimpses of the old him that I'd known growing up. Not the stoic and closed off new Greyson, but the one that had more fun than anyone out on the ice. Maybe he hadn't changed at all, maybe it was my presence that caused him to act icy.

18 GREY-PRESENT

It felt like someone was repetitively stabbing me. Her being called "mom," stab one. Her being a seemingly concerned mom who loves her kid, the exact kind of mom I knew she'd be, stab two. That kid not being mine, stab three. Me realizing I still to this day wished like hell that could've been my kid, stab four. Her jumping at the sound of my voice like it freaked her out, stab five.

And now, running drills with her son who'd been a part of her life for pretty much the same amount of time that I had.

It was painful, but at the same time, something about it felt right.

Her son was good. He was a speedy little guy. His skating skills were definitely advanced for his age. But the advantage he had over the other kids was kind of deadpanned with his lack of hands. The kid desperately needed some work when it came to his stickhandling and shooting.

That's what I told myself when I'd singled him and his buddy Troy out to work with.

In the back of my mind, I really wanted to know the kid. I wanted to see if he took after her.

He was a cute kid, that much I could tell through his helmet. He had light freckles scattered on his cheeks and nose and clear blue eyes- the exact shade as Jules. His hair was the same chestnut brown she used to have as a teen.

He'd definitely inherited her love for the ice and her quiet demeanor as well.

He didn't talk much, but rather, listened closely to every word I said, even when his buddies were goofing off and chirping at each other.

She'd raised a good boy. But I guess credit would be due to the kid's father as well… who I had yet to see… and who I did not want to see.

I decided then that I wouldn't harbor any ill feelings toward her kid… but I couldn't let go of the grudge I held against her for taking all of this away from me… because she ruined me. I looked into her eyes so many years ago and she owned me. I couldn't see starting a family with anyone else and I resented the fact that she could. One part of me wanted to scream at her, but the other part of me knew I never could.

The last fifteen minutes of practice, I had the kids scrimmage and Smitty and I helped our respective teams. I jokingly played defense, and let players by me almost every time, except when Smitty tried to showboat. I shut that down real quick.

But it was a damn good time. I got a kick out of the kids. I purposely wanted to let them all score because I loved watching their over-the-top cellys- what hockey players called celebrations after goals. They'd mature out of that too quickly and play it cool after scoring all too soon. Now was the time to play for the sake of fun and joy, and the celly's showed it.

I also laughed out loud, more like cackled, when I saw them try to hoist their little bodies over top of the boards like the big guys. They'd promptly fall straight down onto the ice, rarely on their feet. One kid got smart and decided to lay his stomach down on the team box boards and throw his feet down first. It became a trend after that.

When the final practice buzzer went off, all the kids scrambled off the ice except two, who stayed behind to help Smitty and I pick up all the pucks and bring the water bottles back to the locker room. It didn't surprise me that one of those kids was Canyon.

Walking out of the cool rink and into the hot fall day hit me with a funny feeling of nostalgia. It was like having a cold sweat for an hour, but not realizing it until just that second. It was a feeling you had to experience because words could never fully give it to you. I used to live for that feeling of walking into the heat knowing that I just had a solid practice. I think that's why Jules and I got along so well as kids. We could talk about stuff like that and really understand each other.

I strolled to my car, thinking that I needed another cup of Tim Horton's coffee, when I heard yelling coming from behind the row of cars in front of me.

I should've kept moving, but against my better judgement, I slowed my pace and started studying the pavement as I strained to hear.

"He is not improving! I told you, we need to send him to St. Jude's. I'm through with this bullshit!" A voice snarled.

I couldn't hear the other side of the argument. It was spoken in too softly of a voice. St. Jude's was a boarding school that was known for athletics. Most of the wealthy families around here shipped their little athlete tykes there. They did have a stellar record of placing kids at D1 universities and they were a great school, but St. Jude's was about three hours south of Northfield.

I told myself I was only concerned with listening because I needed to know if I was losing one of my players. I looked to see which parents were arguing, but they were blocked by the cars. I didn't want to move around the cars and risk the chance of exposing myself as a creep who listened in on private conversations. But in my defense, they were arguing very publicly.

"I'm not going to sit back and watch my kid fuck up all season," the angry voice snapped. I wracked my brain to place the voice but couldn't. And on top of that, all of the kids who made the cut for the team were pretty damn good for their age…

"He is not going there! And I'd like you to stop bringing it up. I have custody. I have the final say."

I knew that voice.

But the words were spoken in a tone that I'd never heard out of her mouth before. I detected a slight shake in her voice even though she had obviously tried to sound firm.

I heard a snide laugh in return and my gut twisted.

"You stupid, stupid bitch," he countered.

Those words shocked me like an ice bucket dumped down my back, and my body stopped walking altogether.

"You have custody because I allowed it. I can bury you in court and make you look like the loony bitch you are."

I felt like the breath had been knocked out of me and I couldn't move. Those words hurt me, so I couldn't imagine what they did to her. I couldn't believe that an hour ago I had wanted to scream at her. What did that say about me?

I shook my head. I was in the right in our situation. What she did to me was wrong.

But she wasn't what this man, who was obviously Canyon's jackass father, was calling her.

I heard a car door slam coming from that direction, signaling the end of the argument.

I tried to shake what I'd just heard out of my head, but I couldn't.

I wanted to go over to her and demand answers. What the hell was that? How could he talk to her like that?

And how could she possibly have loved him more than me?

I heard the car ignition then, and a moment later saw Jules' profile in a Ranger Rover leaving the parking lot.

19 GREY – 9 YEARS AGO

There was ringing in my ears. Loud. I put my hands up to my ears to stop it, but it wouldn't work.

I was blinking hard, as hard as I could, wondering if I was blinded.

I slowly came to the realization that it was just pitch-black outside and the car was completely dead.

The ringing in my ears was painful as fuck.

I took stock of my limbs; the car was crunched close to me but I could still move everything.

But my head. It hurt so fucking bad. My vision was swimming, like I was underwater.

And then I remembered where I was going and who I was with.

Panic swelled inside of me like I'd never experienced before, and I started shaking so hard I couldn't unbuckle. I could see she was unconscious in the seat next to me and her seat belt had been on. I was afraid to move her. Hockey had taught me that much. You never wanted to move someone who possibly had a neck injury and risk making it worse.

Oh God, what if she had a neck injury. What if I hurt her? I cried out, incapable of any true words.

Searching for a way out of my stuck seatbelt I felt something wet and sticky on my hands. Looking down and focusing my eyes as hard as I could, I saw red. A lot of it.

She stirred then and I paused.

She looked over at me and shock registered on her face.

"Greyson!" She cried and reached to touch me.

I didn't care what she said or how she said it, just hearing her speak and seeing her move put me at ease and darkness closed around me.

I blinked against the starch white brightness and tried to bring my hand to my eyes, but I couldn't. My arms felt like lead.

I felt a woman's hand was in mine. Thank God. Jules was okay.

I tried to mutter "Jules," but I choked instead.

The darkness started to close in around me and I let my body fall back into it. I was so tired.

This time when I woke up, there wasn't a hand in mine. I missed it and wondered where Jules had gone. She was probably somewhere near, bossing a nurse or doctor around. She wouldn't leave me here alone.

This time I was able to push myself up.

I looked around and noticed Max's mom sleeping in the corner of the room.

But then the darkness got me again.

The next time I awoke I was up for good. I felt like shit. But I was alive and could move.

Nurses were immediately zooming around me, and a doctor appeared in my room within minutes. He spoke to me so quickly I couldn't understand what he was saying. My head was still killing me so much that I couldn't focus. The side of my face was aching. It felt like I'd been hit with a hammer. I reached to touch it and found it bandaged. I couldn't wait until he left the room so I could ask Max's mom for a recap. It felt like I'd been slammed a couple hundred times into the boards.

I'd been asleep for two days.

But I walked away from the wreck with a concussion, a burst

eardrum that would heal in time and a deep gash in my face from a shard of the windshield. That was where all the blood had come from. It would leave a scar, but I didn't give a shit. I only cared about Jules and no one would tell me what happened to her or how she was doing and it pissed me off. She hadn't been here. The hand had been Max's Mom's.

I wasn't allowed out of my room until I was cleared, but I didn't do well with rules restraining me.

After an hour of waiting and going crazy on my own I roared at a nurse to tell me where the fuck my girlfriend was and I'm pretty sure she peed her pants. She exited quickly and Max and Paige entered.

I didn't like the look on their faces. I didn't like it one bit.

She was alive. I'd seen her awake and moving. But fear bubbled inside of me that something happened after I'd fallen unconscious.

If Jules was gone, I couldn't go on. She had to be in this world with me. And taking her from this world… It couldn't be my fault. It just couldn't.

"What?" I spat at them.

They were still silent and not looking at me. I felt the rage building in me.

"Tell me!" I roared and slammed my fist on the bed, making the IV stand fall down.

"Shit. Easy, man," Max said as he leaned down to pick up the IV. "They're going to commit you or somethin' if you don't mellow out." Max spoke in an even voice that sounded like it was coming from underwater and it wasn't doing anything to calm my nerves at all.

"She's okay," Paige told me then and I felt like I could finally breathe. "But… she's not here," she finished. "We don't exactly know where she is," Paige's eyes were darting around the room nervously. She wouldn't make eye contact with me.

"What the fuck does that even mean?" I asked. Paige flinched at my harsh tone.

Max gave her an apologetic look and stepped in front of her, "It means her grandaddy came here and raised hell and got her taken to a better hospital. She was in a coma. Just like you were."

I felt rage twisted with disgust. He didn't understand that she already chose me. I needed to hold her and to know everything was ok and to tell her how extremely sorry I was. It was all my fault. If

I'd handled it differently everything would've been okay. God. How did everything go so wrong?

"She's moving with me to Texas," I told them. "As soon as we can."

Paige looked at me with a doubtful expression and Max patted my leg on the bed with a sordid expression.

"What?" I demanded.

"Her Pops was…saying stuff about you. He blames you," Max said with a shrug. "I would just focus on yourself and healing for a little while before things cool down, man."

I'd focus on healing, but only with Jules. I needed to get out of this place and find my girl.

I rode the elevator in the "fancier" hospital to her room. The last week had been excruciating.

"Congratulations, baby."

I replayed her saying it over and over again in my mind and it made me want to cry like a damn baby.

She was still asleep. She hadn't woken up since they brought her in.

It didn't make sense to me. We'd both been awake in the car. She screamed when she saw my bleeding face. They told me that was what adrenaline did though, and once it had done its job and the shock wore off, her body had to shut down.

I found out from Paige that she was at Northfield's Mercy Hospital and that she'd had a spinal concussion. She'd probably be fine when she woke up…. she just needed to wake up.

I needed to help her somehow. To hold her and see her and beg her not to leave me.

I could still feel her hair, her smooth skin, how she shivered in the mornings and cuddled closer to me, wanting me to protect her. I needed to help her and give her warmth.

But he wouldn't let me.

The man was the devil in my mind.

I tried to see her every single day of the last week and every single day I was escorted away from the room.

She was laying there, lost in space and not knowing that I cared about her enough to hold her hand and that tore me to pieces.

Which was why I was trying again today.

I probably looked like hell. I still had the side of my face bandaged, but on top of that I hadn't shaved or even looked in a mirror since I was released a week ago. Jules would've yelled at me to take a shower. I didn't care without her.

I stared at the elevator numbers ticking up until it reached floor five.

When I walked out of the elevator, I was met with two hospital security guards.

They'd been expecting me.

"We're sorry, but you can't come on this floor, Mr. Scott." The guard said with a resigned sigh.

I had so much anger coursing through me, I couldn't see straight. I felt myself shaking and I took a swing at one of the beefy guys.

But my reflexes were still off from being concussed and he quickly restrained me, pinning my arm against my back, and shoving me back into the elevator.

Feeling useless and lost, I backed against the rough brick wall of the hospital and slid down to my butt. I dropped my head in my hands and cried until I made myself physically sick. I dry heaved on the grass next to me for what felt like an hour.

The next two days I spent in the waiting room. If she woke up, she'd ask for me and I wanted to be around.

But not even that was okay with Henry fucking Hurley. He had me banned from the hospital, claiming I was a stalker and who was trying to hurt his granddaughter.

I tried to argue against his charges, but his money proved more powerful than anything I could say… as per usual.

20 JULES – 9 YEARS AGO

I would've been moving to Texas with him around this time.

But he wanted nothing to do with me.

And honestly, I wanted nothing to do with life anymore.

It was amazing to think of how things could go so well just to turn so ugly.

I stared at the new walls around me. My chosen prison. It's not like my grandparents forced me to stay here or anything. I just had no desire to get up and move. Life had just turned completely upside down on me. I figured my life would be set at this point- moving in with Greys, getting a job I loved... Instead, I had nothing.

I guess I deserved what I was going through. I'd had it so wonderful with Greys for six years while most of the other girls in my grade were single. But now I'd be single forever because I would never give my heart to someone like that again.

I hated him. I was disgusted by him.

But...

Deep down….

I would take him back in a second if he would only ask to be forgiven. The thought of a phone call brought tears to my eyes. I wanted it so badly. Only, I hadn't heard from him since that text…

I'd woken up in the hospital alone.

My grandparents showed up a couple of hours later. They were on a business trip. That was jarring in and of itself- while their only granddaughter was lying in a hospital bed, they decided it would be okay to go on with business.

While I waited for them, I begged the nurse to let me see Grey, but she had no idea who I was talking about.

Surely he'd come and try to see me. He loved me and I was in the hospital.

A doctor came in and asked me how I was feeling and if I remembered what had happened to me.

It dawned on me then that I didn't. I had no recollection of what had happened that landed me in the hospital. But I knew that Grey would want to know where I was. He'd probably feel bad that he wasn't here with me. He was probably worried he hadn't heard from me… in…I don't even know how long… I didn't know how long I'd been here… I tried to calm my breathing…

Maybe he didn't know that I was even in the hospital?

I asked the nurse for my phone but she just shrugged and said I wasn't admitted with one.

That was odd too. It was always on me.

When my grandparents came into the room, I immediately asked them about Grey, but they ignored my questions and talked over me.

"My phone," I said loudly to break through their discussion.

My grandfather gave me an exasperated look, "what about it, Julianna?"

I cleared my throat, "I need one please. Mine's gone."

My grandfather then lifted his phone to his ear and barked into it for someone to get me a phone as he walked out of the door.

That was the last I'd seen of him in the hospital.

The new phone was lying next to me when I awoke the next morning.

A lot of my info had already been transferred to this one, which made things easier.

I quickly noticed unread messages from Grey and that immediately put me at ease.

Until I read them.

Nothing could have prepared me…

Jules, I am sorry to say this, but we are not good for each other. I cannot be with you anymore. I'm just holding you down and I'm going to get really busy this year with hockey. I hope you are well, and I wish you the best.

I'm so sorry for what happened. You deserve better. I can't get past knowing what I did to you.

Like… what the hell? It didn't even sound like him. And what he 'did to me'? Made me love him? What was he even talking about? He always texted that he loved me and he never once took the time to capitalize I's in his texts. And now not even a goodbye or anything. I thought it was a joke at first, but I'd texted and called him like crazy since I read it and I'd received nothing back. I was so in shock I think I was actually numb and not really believing it. I figured, okay, maybe he got scared or something and moving in was too fast for him and he'd call me in a couple of days… but the call never came.

Instead, I'd only received one more text that read: *"You need to stop. This is over."*

I felt like I'd been slapped across the face.

And that just brought rage.

He was trying to make it look like I was crazy? He was the one who had just asked me to move in with him and now he was breaking up with me over text messages. Of course I was going crazy. Who wouldn't? I didn't even know what to make of that.

So, I tried Paige. But nothing, the calls weren't even being answered. I figured she couldn't face it to tell me that Greyson was done with me. I couldn't blame her. I wouldn't want to be the one to tell her if Max ever decided he didn't want her anymore. And maybe she'd turned on me as well…

So, my everyday turned into tears. I cried for him. Cried for me. Cried over stupid shit we'd done or said. We'd been together for so long that everything had a memory attached to him.

How do you go from talking to someone every day and from them being your center to having them just gone?

Every morning I hoped to see a stupid goofy good morning text from him like usual, but it never came. He had texted me good morning for the past six years… and that was something I missed the most. How pathetic was I?

Everything changed when I was in that stupid hospital bed. The life I thought I was going to have had been ripped away from me and what replaced it was a weird fog of a life that I didn't want.

My grandparents arranged for me to move into our cottage in the Hamptons where they'd be for the rest of the summer, so they could supposedly "look after me as I recovered."

I hated the loneliness of the Hamptons. I'd only ever gone for a week at a time in the past because I was usually training all summer and because Greyson was never allowed to come with me. I had no excuse to avoid it anymore. But I had to face it: I had no plans or job. The Hamptons with my grandparents was my only choice.

I locked myself in my designated room all July, not even bothering to finish job applications or even step onto the ice to fulfill coaching commitments that I'd previously signed on for. I couldn't do it. Everything reminded me of him and of what I'd lost- my whole life with him. I wanted to marry him and have babies with him and have every night and every morning with him. And now I had nothing. I was lost in a void that didn't make any sense.

I knew in the back of my mind I'd never love anyone else.

It was a hopeless mantra I repeated all day, every day. I couldn't give my heart to anyone else. My heart was with him, and I needed to accept that.

I told myself I needed to stop being pathetic and to embrace hatred for him. He didn't even fight for us. He just killed everything we had. But I couldn't get over it. I couldn't seem to accept that as an answer.

My love and hate for him were becoming intertwined. I couldn't get past the fact that I was strong before he came along. Maybe not happy, but independent. He was the one that interjected himself into my life. Why do that if you knew you'd be leaving?

I thought I had hit my lowest; I really, truly did.

But then came my grandparents fucking Labor Day party and things went from bad to way way worse.

– – – –

"Honey, you look lovely!" My grandmother crooned. Gag. She hadn't asked me once in the past month if I was okay. I was just a pain to her.

"And this, Kevin, is my granddaughter, Julianna," my granddad proudly said to a tall stranger. "Kevin is a promising guy in the office," he said with a wink.

Kevin leaned forward from behind my granddad to shake my hand and my granddad gave me a not-so-inconspicuous grin and raised his eyebrows as if to say- he's a good prospect. It made me sick. They were foaming at the mouths at the idea of handing me off to anyone who wasn't Greyson.

I gave a tight-lipped polite smile and shook his hand. It was easy to notice he was tall and handsome and probably around 28-30, but not my type at all. He had the slicked back hair and grin that said, 'I know I'm good looking,' topped off with all the high-end brand clothes and a huge ass watch that screamed money man. I'd been around this type of guy my whole life. The kind my granddad liked. Everything that Greyson was not.

But I couldn't help but think, how easy it would be- to date someone and it not being a fight every time their name was mentioned. To not feel tense and afraid of what both parties would say whenever a holiday or family event came up.

But he was no Grey. Grey's eyes danced excitedly and mischievously, like he was always one fun step ahead of you; like he had some great surprise in store just for you. Kevin's eyes were practically black and flat, and his smile was fake, and his hand was meaty and gross- definitely not that of a skilled athlete.

"Would you like a drink?" He asked with a sly smile, while looking me up and down.

Fuck it. He was probably a harmless business snooze.

"I'd love about five," I said dryly. My grandparents laughed like I was being funny. Eat your hearts out, I thought, and I let Kevin lead me away to the bar.

That was my first mistake. But I didn't keep count, considering I did have about five drinks.

With Grey, I loved to be tipsy. He'd be so sweet, letting me lean on him and he'd brushing his hands through my hair. He'd lean down and kiss my head every couple of minutes, and I couldn't wait to get back to his bed and cuddle with him.

But maybe that was what being young and in love was like- exciting and safe and fun. Feeling jittery at the prospect of getting to spend the night together. Loving looking at him and brushing my thumb under his eye. Feeling so lucky to be together.

Maybe because I wasn't so young anymore, I'd never have it that way again. I'd never feel so absolutely loved and free.

Maybe our love had only been fueled by innocence. We experienced all our firsts together: loving, drinking, sex, it was all exciting. Maybe it would've been exciting to experience all of that with anyone?

Or maybe that was how the world worked. The people who got

lucky were the ones who stayed with their first love. They were able to keep that innocent and pure kind of love that made you blind to all faults. They felt that happy drunk on life young euphoria with that special first love and were able to keep it. Did everyone else just pick someone and decide to settle with them and all their "love" was just a lie?

That thought made me want to drink even more. I figured if I was drunk enough, maybe I wouldn't be so sad, and maybe I wouldn't care that my new place would be next to a guy like this instead of Greyson.

Kevin led me around the party proudly. I nodded and smiled when I had to.

He knew exactly what to say to everyone. No coaching needed. No making side jokes at the rest of the party's expense. He was a mingling pro. I didn't open my mouth once and I think he preferred it that way.

He kept giving me sly smiles and looking down my dress. Whatever. It was easier to get drunk with him than with my grandparents. I tried to make it okay in my head. He wasn't bad looking. He had a good job.

But then he leaned to whisper in my ear, "Want to get out of here?"

Did I? Yes. Did I want to leave with him specifically? No. Did I enjoy his breath on my ear? Definitely not.

I looked for my grandparents then. They were fake laughing with a bunch of other preppishly dressed old-timers. They didn't even care to look for me. No one cared about me anymore.

I couldn't help but think about the fact that my grandparents didn't want me with Grey, when he always looked out for me and everything we did was always safe… how would they feel about me going all out with Kevin?

I looked back at Kevin and nodded.

I needed to force myself into the next season of my life.

21 GREY - PRESENT

For the first game of the season, Max gifted Smitty and I clipboards and warned us not to break them in front of the kids. His dad was our coach for u16 and 17 and he broke about a hundred each year in anger. I couldn't help but laugh, Smitty and I were super laid back, no danger there.

Smitty took a backseat when it came to coaching. He liked hanging with the kids during practices and watching the games from the bench, but he didn't want to make any decisions regarding the actual hockey part. This worked out well because I was finding I loved it and comfortably slid into the head coach slot.

While I was hesitant on taking the job and figured I probably wouldn't even learn a single kid's name through the season- I had planned on calling them by their numbers- I surprised myself by really getting into the game and even using their little nicknames that I'd picked up on at practice.

Canyon was playing center on my first line. He earned it. He'd had about five breakaways, busting through the play and skating all the way down the ice, but missed the net by a long shot each time. He was like a little energizer bunny. He zoomed around the ice, but then almost had too much energy to focus a shot at the end.

I needed to work with him on finishing business. We'd dominate the season if he could score on even a couple of his breakaways.

We won the game 5-0, and Max came up on the bench and gave

us both a congratulatory slap on the back and said beers after the game were on him-as long as we went to Benny's.

I slid onto the ice in my Nikes behind my team and tapped all the little kids gloves and shook the opposing coaches' hands. The kids all looked at me with a gleam in their eyes, probably noticing that I'd been in the NHL just last year. All of my kids quickly lost that gleam and became rugrats at the second practice, which was better with me.

I'd gotten so into the game, that I'd completely forgotten about the locker room part.

The part where mostly dads came in and helped their kid unlace their skates and change.

I must've gotten used to seeing Canyon with only Jules in the locker room because it was like a punch to the gut when I saw a stranger with slicked back hair kneeling in front of Canyon.

I let Smitty do the honors of a post-game chat. So much anger and aggression was coursing through me that I could hear the blood pumping in my ears. If I spoke to the kids now I'd probably scare the shit out of them. I could see myself ripping him away from Canyon and beating the hell out of him. Instead, I just pulled my cap low and sat back silently assessing him.

I'd seen him before but I couldn't place where.

The guy looked like he'd just walked off Wall Street rather than from the bleachers of a youth hockey game. He was all business, dressed in a suit and had a slight tan, a bit overkill for September. Honestly, he looked like a stuck-up pussy. A try-hard. He had a huge watch on his wrist, purposely worn. He wanted to show off.

I realized, I probably hadn't seen him before, but the resemblance was ridiculous. He was a mini Henry Hurley.

I could tell he was ignoring what Smitty was saying, and he was talking to Canyon. I couldn't hear what he was saying, but it wasn't good by the look on Canyon's dropped down head.

I was grinding my teeth so hard they could crack. I couldn't sit there any longer watching him unlace Canyon's skates. I silently exited the room while Smitty was still talking with the kids

I plopped down in front of Paige and ripped off my hat to give myself a head massage.

"You don't look like a coach who just won," Paige chided as she handed me a cup of coffee.

I glanced at her briefly before taking a sip, "thanks."

"Gonna tell me what's wrong or do I have to guess?"

I looked around Benny's. The place wasn't too busy. It was a more popular post-game dinner spot. Only old geezers, probably there to watch grandsons, dotted the booths in the mornings.

I turned back to see an expectant Paige.

"Did you see who she married?" I asked her incredulously. I couldn't help but say it with disgust.

She raised her eyebrows at me, "So, this is about jealousy? No, I haven't."

The way she responded pissed me off. I had the right to be upset. Jules threw me out all those years ago for that prick?

"There's no need to be jealous," Paige said, almost reading my mind. "They're divorced," she pointed out.

I'd be lying if I said that didn't make me feel a little better to hear. But it was still shit. It was like I was beat in the semi-finals, and seeing my victor lose in the final game. Cool consolation, but I still lost.

I was not looking forward to dealing with what looked like Henry Hurley part two all season. I just hoped he wouldn't show for many of the games, which I knew in the back of my mind was wishing a shit father on Canyon… not what I'd want either. I hoped he at least pretended to be a good dad to him.

I let out a frustrated growl, I didn't know what I wanted anymore.

I knew I needed to talk to her, but I couldn't seem to make it past two sentences before I let anger overtake me and I had to walk away. What we'd had was love. And I couldn't get that with anyone else. Every time I'd tried with anyone else, their touch would feel awkward and unnatural and a picture of her would slam into my mind like the biggest fucking cockblock of all time.

Yeah, I'd been with other girls since her. But I hadn't been intimate with anyone else. I couldn't cross that line. There was sex. But no talking, no foreplay, no cuddling. I could get away with it because those girls had only cared that I was playing in the NHL.

She must not have felt the same about us and I couldn't comprehend it. How had she moved on so easily? She'd gotten married. She took it further with someone else. They had a kid together. I guessed that was just another way she was too good for me.

Smitty arrived then and slapped me on the back so hard I almost lost my sip on the bar.

"We put together quite the team, man. You gotta work with that kid though," he said, shaking his head.

"Which kid?"

"Jules' kid! Didn't you see him out there? Straight fire, then flub."

"Why don't you work with him, you're just as much responsible," I pointed out. I wanted to work with him, I just didn't like being told I had to. "And why aren't we calling him 77? Or Canyon?" I spat out.

"Dude, I'm better with defense." He rolled his eyes, "And like it or not, that's who he is. I'd call him by his last name like the rest of the kids, but I think you'd lose your shit."

I shot him a look that could murder, "fuck you."

I guess I knew who I'd be working with next practice… Jule's kid. In the back of my mind, I knew I was going to help him anyway.

22 JULES - PRESENT

I could tell Canyon wasn't happy when he walked into the lobby struggling under the weight of his bag. While his friends ran to the concession stand, he came straight to me and dumped his bag by my feet. His chest was heaved up and it looked like tears were threatening to come, but he was trying to hide it like hell from the other kids.

"I think Coach Grey's mad I didn't score. Dad is."

I pulled his head toward me into a hug. That concerned me.

"What do you mean, hun? You played a great game," I said, ruffling his hair. "We'll just work on your shot in the driveway, okay?"

He pulled away from me.

"But Mom, you're just a figure skater. You don't know how to do it either," his eyes looked at me helplessly.

"We can figure it out together, bud," I told him, holding his chin, but I'd be lying if this didn't break my heart a little. This was the disadvantage of him living with me full time and Kevin barely coming around. Although, even when Kevin was around, he didn't take much notice of Canyon. He never helped him, yet he was so quick to criticize him.

"Where is your dad?" I felt my anxiety rise as I scanned the lobby.

"He left. He said I needed to work on actually scoring," Canyon was lightly kicking his bag with his toe and didn't want to look up at me. My sweet boy. He never wanted anyone to see him tear up. He was fighting it back.

"Know what else is bad," Canyon struggled out, "Coach Grey was mad at me too. Do you think he won't like me anymore because I didn't score?"

I bent down to him then and looked into his worried little eyes, "No, baby. He wasn't mad, sometimes you just can't get one in."

"He didn't say anything to me after the game and he had a mad face on," He grimaced.

"Baby," I held his little jaw. "I know Coach Grey from when we were kids, he didn't score all the time either," I said.

"You knew him?" He asked with widened eyes.

"Yupp. Remember I skated here too? So I know he wasn't mad at you about that. He had a season where he couldn't even get one point, let alone goal," I forced out a wry smile to make my baby feel better.

He widened his eyes at that and then he asked me for five bucks for a slushy, so I think I'd eased his little mind on the matter. I wasn't as easily satisfied though. Was Greyson actually mad at my kid for not scoring?

Leaving the rink, I lifted Canyon's bag for him and we headed out together.

Grey's figure cast a shadow on the cement stairs leading down to the parking lot. He was watching Canyon and I approach through his sunglasses. I hated those damn sunglasses. Grey used to be so easy to read. We used to joke that he'd never be able to gamble because his poker face was so utterly horrible. I wondered if I'd still be able to read him, but I couldn't tell because his hat and sunglasses took away any ability I'd have anyway. I still wasn't sure how we were supposed to interact with each other either. Were we supposed to forget the past and just move forward? It was a hard pill to swallow knowing that the bubbly guy that was my person and loved me with everything he had turned into this stoic figure looking back at me with a stony face. God, he still looked the same though. I always wondered if he knew he had every woman looking at him when he entered a room.

We'd said about two sentences to each other so far, and I honestly wondered if we'd speak again all season.

He gave me a curt nod, and I nodded politely back.

When we hit the bottom step, I heard him call out.

"7's," he said.

Canyon was number 77.

Canyon turned back towards him, holding up his hand with his slushy in it to cover his eyes. Grey was standing in front of the sun as he walked down the stairs toward us.

"C'mere bud."

I backed away a bit, giving them some space. I guessed this was a coaching moment of some sort. I figured it was needed, considering my kid thought he was mad at him.

He bent his large frame down, his knees cracking as he lowered himself to canyon's level and he whispered to him. I stole the moment to study his face. His strong jawline that I used to kiss appeared more prominent than when we were young… but the thing I couldn't get past was that scar. It bugged me that I didn't know this part of him.

Canyon was nodding with a serious look on his face. They fist bumped each other then and Canyon bounded over to me.

Grey gave me another nod behind those sunglasses.

"I need my bag, Mom," Canyon told me.

"Uh, ok. Did you forget something?"

"No, I mean I need to carry it."

"That's okay hun, I got it

"No, I hafta," he seemed to puff out his chest then. "Coach said that real men don't have their moms carry their bags for them. He said dad shoulda taught me that already." He looked up at me for verification, but I was stunned. Even if Kevin was a jerk, Grey didn't know that. He had no place criticizing Kevin… and in extension, me. He was criticizing my choice. Well. He could eat his heart out. It was not my choice, and he took himself out of the running.

I turned back towards Grey, and he was staring right at me, holding my gaze, as if he were challenging me. I could see his jaw throbbing. He gave a brisk nod and turned back to the rink.

23 JULES - PRESENT

Canyon and I made breakfast every Sunday morning together.

I was already sipping some coffee and making pancake mix when he entered the kitchen in his pjs. He sleepily pulled a chair over to the counter where I was mixing the batter and he silently added chocolate chips to it while rubbing his eyes.

The kid knew our routine so well he could do it practically sleeping.

I laughed and kissed his head.

My phone rang, interrupting my stirring. I quickly wiped my hands off on my sweatpants and grabbed up my phone. It was an unknown number calling.

"Hello?"

"Hullo," a gravelly voice replied.

I knew that greeting. He didn't even have to say his name. Excluding his father, Greyson was the only person I knew who changed his e's to u's in saying hello. My teenage self got a kick out of it. Now it made my chest feel tight.

"Grey?" Saying his name aloud after all these years felt so foreign. It had been a word I omitted from my vocabulary, not to be uttered.

That perked the little man's ears up, and he immediately looked at me with interest as he shoved a handful of chocolate chips into his mouth.

There was a pause on the other end of the line.

"Yeah," he drawled out. "I was just calling because… Canyon."

"Oh. You want to talk to him? He's right here," I supplied.

It still felt so odd to hear his voice on the other end of the phone. I'd wanted it more than anything else for years. But instead of the comfort I used to get from his voice, it now brought shaky nerves. I'd be happy to pass off the phone call to my son to give myself some time to get used to this new dynamic, but I couldn't handle it if he was going to be taking digs at my life choices to my son.

"Can you keep it to hockey?" I said tightly.

There was a pause on the other end of the line.

"Yes," He breathed out.

I handed the phone to Canyon and gave a shrug.

"Coach?" He mouthed to me with wide eyes, and I nodded.

"Coach Grey?" Canyon asked into the phone.

I couldn't hear the other end of the line, but Canyon happily chatted away with him, so I continued the pancake making process.

A couple minutes later, he got down from his chair and went to peak in the garage.

"Yeah, we got it here," I heard Canyon say.

Canyon wandered back into the kitchen and handed me my phone.

"Good chat?" I asked him, to which he nodded vigorously. He took his spot back on the counter and watched me pour the batter onto the griddle.

Right when I was handing him the first three pancakes, the doorbell rang, causing me to almost drop them.

I took in a deep breath. I didn't think Kevin was coming over to see Canyon today. I did not want to have to gear myself up to see him. I hoped it was just Jen asking us to watch Troy.

"That's for me!" Canyon announced and raced for the door, cutting off my thoughts

"Wait, Canyon who is that?" I called to him.

"Coach!" He called.

"What?!" I asked with alarm in my voice.

Canyon stopped in his tracks halfway to the door and looked at me like I was crazy, "I thought you said I could invite friends over."

I continued to stare at my kid who didn't have all the pieces to connect that he'd just invited my ex over.

"I can't tell him not to come now, Mom. He's gonna help me with my shot! He's already here!" He protested.

"Uh.. okay, I guess," he did have a point, but I was having trouble grasping the concept that Canyon considered Greyson Scott his friend.

I couldn't see the front door from my place in the kitchen, but I could hear as Canyon opened the door.

"Hey, bud," I heard Grey say to Canyon.

"Mom's making pancakes. Want some? I put extra chocolate."

"You sure she wouldn't mind?" Grey's deep voice asked him.

"She didn't know you were coming, and she was a little mad about it, but we always have extras," he told him. I internally groaned. My son, the truth teller.

I found myself feeling shaky all of a sudden in picturing myself from Grey's eyes. Almost ten years older, in my ratty jogger sweatpants and a ragged cut off t-shirt with my hair piled on top of my head in a messy bun with only traces of eye makeup leftover from yesterday. Great. He was going to think I peaked at 22. I tried to remind myself that it didn't matter anyway. He was here for Canyon, not me.

He'd had enough of me a long time ago and he never looked back. I shouldn't either. I busied myself with dumping more batter onto the griddle.

"Hullo,"

I looked up at him. He was in basketball shorts and a Griffins dry-fit short sleeve t-shirt and socks. Greyson Scott had taken his shoes off at my door. What a weird turn in life. He looked uncomfortable standing there at the edge of my kitchen, not making eye contact with me. All thoughts of a grudge went out the window when I saw him. It was the same when we were kids. I'd be mad at him, but as soon as I looked up at him and saw his face, half the anger would dissipate- I hated it at times- but he had that effect on me. He was such a large guy, but half the time he looked like a lost puppy that only needed a little affection to be so happy.

"Uh, hi," I forced a smile, reminding myself he was here to help Canyon. "Want some?"

"Sure, always up for free food," he said quietly. Still looking unsure he made his way towards the kitchen table where Canyon was pouring syrup on his pancakes.

"My mom makes the best ones," Canyon told him. "They're much better than restaurant ones… or Tammy's," he said, making a yuck face.

"Canyon, be nice," I warned, but I couldn't help but stifle a laugh. My bud was always on my side.

Tammy was Kevin's girlfriend.

"I gag when I eat at Tammy's," I heard Canyon whisper and then look at me through the corner of his little eyes, making sure that I heard it.

"Your uh, Mom's pancakes have always been good," Grey said, sounding uneasy.

"You've had them?" Canyon asked curiously.

I found myself trying to stay busy in the kitchen to avoid eye contact with either of them.

"Many times," Grey's laugh made a low rumble. "She ever put marshmallows in them for you?"

"The little, tiny kind!" Canyon said.

"Yeah," Grey chuckled again. "I taught her that."

I felt my face blush. I focused on looking down because I did not want to meet his gaze.

"She only makes them sometimes for special stuff," Canyon pouted. He imitated me then in a girly voice saying, "ooh! too much sugar!" Which only caused Grey to laugh more. Even after all these years, the sound of his voice stirred something inside of me and I wanted to shut it down.

Wanting to keep myself busy, I started to clean up the batter when I slammed my hip on the corner of my kitchen island. The hit caused me to drop the dirty glass measuring cup and it shattered on the floor next to me. I leaned down and held my hip bone with a wince.

Grey was up in an instant, moving toward me and I saw Canyon start to leave his seat.

"No, honey, there's glass over here, stay put, okay?" I winced.

A second later, I felt a touch on my hip and I jumped away from it, causing a jolt of pain to shoot through me.

A low rumble of a laugh came from behind me, "Easy, it's just me," Grey said with wide eyes, and I felt his warmth move closer to me again.

If only he knew, I thought wryly, and shut my eyes against the throbbing pain. He tried again then, and I let him. His strong, calloused hand rubbed over my right hip bone. If the pain didn't make me feel like crying, the nostalgia did.

"Feel okay?" he said in a low tone.

I swallowed hard. I didn't want his warm grip to leave my body. It felt so safe and calming. How pathetic of me. I had to remind myself he had left me in the dust. Where was my dignity?

"Yeah," I moved away from his grip, but he tried to keep me there a second longer.

"You sure?" he asked. "Hell of a hip check," he joked lightly.

I nodded, avoiding his dark rimmed eyes, and started to grab some paper towels to clean up the glass, moving slow because my hip did still hurt.

"You need some ice?" his dark eyebrows scrunched together in concern. Why was he being so nice to me now? It was easier when he was icy. I didn't want to want him.

"It's okay, thank you," I said politely.

He bent down to help me pick up the large shards of glass.

He caught my eyes then and his jaw twitched, "no glass hit you, right? Leaves a hell of a scar." I looked up to see his face turn to stone once again. Under my gaze he looked away.

I shook my head no, "I can finish this up though. Thank you for…"

He missed a beat and swallowed, "no problem, Jules."

When he returned to his seat, he and Canyon continued talking about the team and I finished up the last batch of pancakes.

I put the last pile in front of them and turned to leave, but the boys wouldn't have it.

"Wait, Jules…" I heard Grey say.

I turned at the edge of the kitchen, sipping my coffee. His eyes looked like they were pleading.

"Hmm?"

"You should eat," His eyes burned holes into me, through me, taking us back to sixteen.

"Yeah, Mom! You can't break tradition," Canyon said.

Grey looked at him curiously, "tradition?"

"Every Sunday we stuff ourselves with pancakes," Canyon said simply.

"Well, I can't be the one breaking a tradition, hockey players take those seriously," Grey smiled at him and then me.

I slowly walked back to the table and took a seat across from the boys then. My stupid stomach chose right then to let a growl out, causing both the boys to start laughing at me. I was hungry…

Maybe this could be our come to peace moment.

24 GREY - PRESENT

When I first saw her in the kitchen, I nearly forgot it had been years since we'd been together. She looked almost the exact same. Her hips were maybe a little wider, and she seemed to have leaned out in other places where she'd lost muscle, but her standing there in that old t-shirt made it feel like we were 22 again. Canyon had said she didn't know I was coming, so she didn't have any time to prepare. But I always loved her like this. Right out of bed, with barely any makeup on so you could see her freckles. She made messy look sexy. And that t-shirt... It was from a country concert that we went to together. I bet she didn't even remember where she'd gotten it. But it made me feel lighter knowing that she still had remnants of our past. I carried one on my face, it only seemed right.

Another thing that nagged me as soon as I saw her: I knew what was under her shirt, and I still wanted it.

When I'd touched her hip, it was like a time warp. I had held her hips so often. I felt the rush of an urge to pick her up, have her wrap her legs around me and make out right there on the counter. I imagined it would feel so natural. So right. I wouldn't be cock blocked with guilt because she was The One. I wanted it so bad. But I had to bring myself back down to this reality.

I wondered if the glass comment had reminded her of how I got the scar she had questioned the other day, but I didn't see anything register in her face. How could she not remember? The fact that she didn't was so fucking painful.

That was a different life ago though. Canyon was a reminder of that. We would have to navigate this new life- the one where she'd married someone else. I felt myself clenching my jaw and forced myself to breathe deeply every time I thought about it. I knew that I had to accept what I'd lost- that she didn't want me back then; but for some reason I couldn't shove it behind me.

I tried to push all my negative thoughts away so I could enjoy having breakfast with her and Canyon.

When she didn't sit down right away to eat with us and appeared to be skipping breakfast, I was tempted to say I wasn't leaving the table until she did eat… something I'd had to do in our past because of her figure skating. If that were the case, then I knew she needed someone. Someone to be watching over her. Someone who really knew her and loved her. I did calm when Canyon said they stuffed themselves every weekend though.

I could be angry with her all day, but at the end of any day, I'd be lying if I said I didn't want to be the someone that she needed or wanted. And that made me so confused. I was so hurt by her but so damn addicted to her even after all these years.

Sitting there, having pancakes with Jules and Canyon, felt right.

I knew now more than ever before that I needed to know what happened all those years ago. Because that's where I was stuck.

Because this should have been all of ours.

Canyon and I sat in the grass next to the driveway putting our rollerblades on.

We were going to run some drills out in their cul-de-sac, she really did have a great place in the neighborhood for street games. Hopefully with a little work I could have Canyon actually hitting the net after his breakaways.

I was wrong about him being quiet though, he was quite the chatterbox. Seemed that once he accepted me, he did not shut up.

I decided to try to steer his conversation a bit to something that had been bugging me.

"So, who's Tammy?" I asked him, thinking she was a babysitter or something.

"That's um…" he grimaced and I felt bad then for changing to a topic he didn't want to discuss.

"I'm sorry, never-" I started.

"My dad's, um, friend?" He asked more than said.

I closed my eyes and had to take a deep breath. I should have known. That guy oozed the title piece of shit.

"Mom's not upset about it," Canyon said quickly. I looked down at him and he looked a little nervous, like he knew she wouldn't want him talking about this. He glanced back at the house. "I don't think they loved each other. They never said it, ya know? They only say I love you to me. I don't want them to live together ever again," he said as firmly as he could.

I had to steady my breathing. Their home life must have been worse than what I was thinking - when even an eight-year-old wanted him away from her. I was about a second from losing my mind and wandering back into the house to ask her what the hell she did in choosing him over me. Why would she have taken such a risk with her life when I could have given her so much more? I didn't want to do it in front of her kid though. I wished like hell I still had hockey as a outlet because I felt the hum of angry energy overtaking my body. I wanted to pummel the guy.

I tried a quick deep breathing exercise that one of my old team's shrinks told me to practice.

When I finished and looked back up, Canyon was already on his feet rolling away, and he yelled back at me, "C'mon Coach!"

As upset as I was with the situation, I also knew I only had control over the now.

After a couple of hours of playing around outside we were drenched in sweat and ready for a break. It was September, but definitely an Indian summer this year- around noon it had to have been about eighty degrees. Playing street hockey with him made me feel like a kid again; like I was completely carefree and weightless, and my only goal was to have fun.

Jules walked out a little bit ago and put two Gatorades and protein bars near our stuff in her front yard and watched us for a couple of minutes.

She looked so casually beautiful, standing there barefoot on her lawn watching her kid with a genuine smile on her face.

It was funny, her presence still made me want to show off. I took a break from teaching for a minute and fooled around, making some quick dekes around the kid and easily shoved one in the net.

I looked back at the house to see her shaking her head with a smile on her face.

Canyon and I were silent as we plopped down to drink and eat our snacks.

"What happened to your face?" Canyon asked me after taking a large bite of his bar.

I laughed mid-swig and almost choked, "what do you mean, kid? That comes off a bit mean," I pointed out before taking a swig of Gatorade.

He made a funny face then and pointed on his face to his eyebrow, and lip, and then cheek- the places I had noticeable scars.

"Well, bud," I laughed again, "I do not scar well. Some people heal up real good, my skin just doesn't."

I pointed to my lip, "this was a stick to the face when I was goofing off with coach Smitty when we were kids. I thought your mom was gonna deck him when she saw what he did to me."

"What?!" Canyon thought that was tremendously funny.

"Yeahhh… she actually bandaged this up. I probably should've gone to the hospital; it might've healed better." I laughed at the memory of her freaking out at me and wanting so badly to take me in. I hated hospitals though.

I pointed to my eyebrow then, "This happened in college hockey- your mom actually saw that one too," I stopped myself then, wondering what kind of relationship Canyon thought his mom and I had in the past. This kind of relationship where she'd kiss me through any kind of gross stitches and not care. His curious frown told me he didn't know much about us. I wasn't sure what I should say exactly about the next scar.

"And this," I felt the gash that ran under my cheek bone. It was half covered by scruff, I kept it that way on purpose. "This happened right after college, not from hockey. I was in a car accident," I grimaced thinking about it.

"Ohh," Canyon said gravely, "my mom knows about those, she was in a bad one too once. Before me."

"She told you about it?" I asked him too quickly, wondering how much he knew- if he knew we'd been together. And that I had been the one driving.

"A little," he said, squinting against the sun. "She doesn't remember any of it though. She said it had to have been real bad because she got knocked out for a while and she said she gets a real bad feeling when she thinks about it."

The kid might as well have dropped a bomb on me. I looked at him in shock.

"Did yours knock you out too?"

I nodded dumbly. That's why she asked me about the scar. She didn't forget it because it was unimportant- she really didn't know what happened. To me. To us. The thought crossed my mind that maybe she could've lied to Canyon about it… but she really didn't seem like the type of mom to lie to her kid. I needed to talk to her. I couldn't wait anymore; I needed to do it today.

I found her in the kitchen working at her laptop. I walked right up to her. Standing in front of her, I looked down at her. She jumped slightly, and I felt bad for scaring her. It was still amazing to me that we were here, finally facing each other again. She shifted uncomfortably.

"Uh, where's Canyon?"

"He's up in his room, I asked him to give us a minute." I reached and pulled her hand to my face. It burned on the scar. She seemed to shrink back a little, but I wouldn't let her remove her hand from mine. Nerves coursed through me making me feel unsteady.

"This scar, you really don't remember what happened?"

"Should I?" Her voice cracked. "Life went on, I get it. Stuff happened to both of us after, Grey. Let's forget it," She pulled her hand from mine and looked unsettled.

"No, you don't get it. This wasn't after us. You were there," I urged.

"No…I wasn't." She eyed me like I was insane. "I would've remembered that."

"Jules. It was from a car accident. Driving back from Brecklin. You helped me pack all day and we were so tired! We were going to live together in Texas, you don't remember?" I pleaded. "You were in an accident too, Canyon told me you remember that. Your accident was right at that time, wasn't it? That summer. Please, think back."

"I… no… I was in an accident, but…." she looked at me in confusion and hurt. "You weren't there Grey."

I felt like I'd been slapped in the face.

"I remember waking up in the hospital alone and scared," she continued shakily, not making eye contact with me. "Not even my grandparents were there, I figured you'd come soon, but you never did. I had no one, and I was scared and I…" She looked at me then, seemingly gaining confidence to raise her voice at me. "I needed you, Grey. And then, when I got my phone back…" her face clouded over. She stood up, pushed past me.

My frustration mounted new levels at that point; never in my life had I felt so helpless. I needed her to understand but it was like we were speaking two different languages at this point. I felt tears sting my eyes, probably the first real tears since I'd lost her all those years ago.

"That hurts me more than I can even say," I struggled out. I was gripping the kitchen counter so hard my knuckles were white. Thinking of her alone in a hospital, not knowing what happened and missing me. And I was right there. I hadn't tried hard enough.

"I was there," I clenched my jaw and shut my eyes, "I was outside that hospital dry heaving on the grass and crying because your grandfather had me banned from the hospital. I was there every day, Jules. Until you left. Then you were completely gone," I paused, not knowing if I should continue. "You know why I can't play anymore?"

She was silent, but then quietly said, "Concussions, right?"

"You saw my first bad one in high school… My second was that accident. And I didn't really take care of myself after that like I should have. It was my own fault. And your granddads. I would have been lying by your side resting the whole time instead of drinking and fighting anyone who came near me and trying like hell to do anything to feel even a little okay. I just wanted to be by your side. You have to know that," I pleaded. "Think back to us, why wouldn't I have wanted to be there? I loved you so damn much."

She backed up against the white pantry wall and scrunched her eyes shut.

"Grey- I just don't-"

I moved to stand across from her then, now too scared to touch her. I waited for her to finish just like I had when we were younger.

"I- I woke up alone. When I got my phone back it had those texts from you."

"Begging to come see you? Yeah, I know, I must've left about a hundred. Probably blubbering and crying-"

"No," She said coldly and looked at me squarely with a strange expression, "you broke up with me. You even told me 'You need to stop. This is over.' Like all those years was nothing. Like I was a child acting up. You know how bad that hurt?"

I opened my mouth, but no words came. It felt like I'd just been punched in the throat.

She seemed to gain power from my silence.

Her face twisted in pain, "I hated you, Grey. I truly hated you. You had no right. No right to take everything from me and say all that you did when everything we had was so empty. I was shattered when you left me. Is that what you wanted to hear? I was content on starting over and forgetting the past, but that's the truth Grey. I hated you and the fact that you could say you loved me so often but then just forget about me and leave. What was I supposed to think?" She snapped.

I was stunned. I felt like I'd been slashed in the gut.

"I never. Julianna. You have got to believe me. I never in a million years would have sent that to you. I just asked you to move with me! I was in love with you!"

She stared at me blankly. She was done, and I felt helpless, but I couldn't stop trying.

"I left so many messages your phone was full! I couldn't leave anymore. I tried like hell to contact you and got nothing back. You just cut me out and left me high and dry. I went to Texas alone ready to murder someone out on the ice because I was so damn depressed."

She covered her mouth with her hand, still staring blankly in front of her.

I reached for her hand and she flinched. That hurt.

"Babe-" I cut myself off. It felt so natural to call her that, it just slipped out. "Sorry." I looked down at her retreating into her thoughts.

"Please, Jules. Ask Paige. She tried like hell to contact you too."

I started to walk away, but I couldn't leave her there in the kitchen staring like that.

"Jules, are you okay? I didn't want-"

Canyon came running down then, and she ran her hands through her hair and gave me a tight-lipped fake smile like the ones she used to give her grandparents. It hurt like hell knowing that she felt the need to put up a front and be fake with me. We were never fake with each other before.

We bared our souls to each other.

How had everything gone so horrendously wrong for us?

"Goodbye, Grey," she told me firmly.

The finality of her statement caused panic to course through me.

25 JULES – 9 YEARS AGO

Fuck. Fuck. Fuck.

Panic welled inside my chest like I'd never experienced before.

I sat there staring at myself in the bathroom mirror. It couldn't be true. It just simply could not.

Looking back at me was a shell of who I used to be. Dark bags under my eyes, hair that needed attention stat, and ribs showing because I'd decided coffee and alcohol would be great staples for a diet. Forget working out or skating. Everything I used to do reminded me of him. I had to avoid it all. Except avoiding it all made me look and feel like absolute shit. There was no way what I saw could be true.

What I saw came with "a glow" and instead it looked like someone stole any light I once had.

My vision blurred then from the tears that immediately came. I cried so hard my body was shaking.

This was not how it was supposed to go. I was supposed to be in Texas with Greyson. Not stuck at one of my grandparents' houses and now crying and having absolutely no one to talk to.

How did Greyson just turn it off? How was he so fine? I streamed his first game tonight and it was torturous. He was playing better than he'd ever before. He looked like he was moving twice as fast as everyone else on the ice.

It was actually surreal. I'd been at almost every one of his important games since high school, and now he was making his AHL debut, a sure highlight in his life… while I was probably at my lowest.

Watching him celebrate with him teammates on my computer screen while I held a pregnancy test cemented that he was in an entirely different world than me now, and that realization made me cry the hardest.

I kept glancing at my phone, wondering if I should try to congratulate him on his game… but what was the point? There was no going back now.

Alone on the floor of my bathroom the grief was finally replaced with twisted hatred. As much as it was my fault for getting with Kevin, I never in a million years would have ever been with him if Grey hadn't abandoned me.

I sought out Kevin for comfort, but in the back of my mind, I knew it wasn't something he could ever give me.

I would never be able to love anyone the way I loved him, and I thought he felt the same way about me. It felt so stable and so real. I could still picture him like he was right there in front of me. The way he looked down at me and said he loved me so quietly; like half of him wanted to say it to me, but half also wanted assurance from me. He'd told me once that he just loved hearing me say it to him. How the hell was that not true love? How could he just walk away from that?

What we had was raw and true and rare. And now it was ruined forever.

He discarded our love like a piece of trash and in doing so, he ruined me. He had no right to make me fall in love with him if he wasn't going to fight for us.

But that's how it was for me. I was never good enough for anyone's love. Not my grandparents, and now not Greyson's either. I just needed to get used to being on my own and I needed to accept that Grey had been it for me.

If only it could be that easy though. He entered and exited my life, but I couldn't disregard all my memories and feelings for him. The way he looked at me and touched me with a gleam of awe and respect making me feel treasured... the way he held me in his arms and comforted me as I cried… the way he pinched my stomach, saying his baby would be there one day.

It was all too much for me.

Because this was Kevin's.

The thought of that broke me.

Greyson would never forgive me.

But who was I kidding? Greyson didn't want me anyway before this. No way would he ever want me now.

A baby.

I touched my stomach.

My grandparents were nowhere to be found. Greyson didn't want me. Kevin wanted me only as a status symbol and possession and didn't really care to have me around unless it was for show.

But I really wasn't alone anymore...and I vowed to myself to never treat my baby with the carelessness that I'd been shown. I needed to keep him. This was my little love to protect.

26 GREY- PRESENT

I stormed into Benny's holding my bleeding hand at a weird angle, trying to stop the blood from staining their floor.

I probably should've driven myself to the hospital, but I couldn't stomach it. I always hated the hospital; it had always been unfriendly to me. As a kid I relied on Jules to help clean me up when I should've gotten stitches. My feelings of hate for the place grew even stronger after losing her. In my mind, I lost her when I was banned and she was lying there unconscious. Throughout my hockey career I was treated by the team docs who knew I would never step foot in a hospital even if they told me to, so they always handled things for me.

My hand probably wasn't even that bad. I figured I was just in a panicked mood and Paige could probably fix it up for me. It just needed some ice. And I needed to ask Paige what to even do about what I'd just learned.

I flinched at the sound of cheers erupting from a group of old timers watching an NHL game. Fuck that. If I couldn't play there's no way in hell I wanted to watch. The anxiety and pain raging inside of me made me want to rip the tv off the wall and slam it onto the ground.

Paige turned the corner and slammed into me, causing me to let out a painful grunt.

"Oh my God, Greyson, what happened?" Her eyes widened and

she looked from my messed-up hand to my face.

I clenched my jaw and looked away.

"I'll get the first aid kit for the bleeding, but that doesn't look okay," Paige said as she ducked behind the counter. "I'm texting Max to come help. You're gonna have to go to the hospital, Grey," she warned. She knew my affinity for the place.

I couldn't get the words out. I was honestly afraid of breaking down. I felt a burning lump of tears waiting to erupt in my throat, making me feel like an eight-year-old kid again, and was rooted to the spot.

"Follow me to the back," she snapped.

Her demand irked me but I needed help. I let out a grunt, trying to clear my throat, and followed her past Benny's kitchen toward the back office. The only times I'd ever been back here were when we were about sixteen or seventeen, horsing around and daring each other to steal beers from the kitchen during summer training days. Things were so much simpler then. It was crazy how back then I had no money or place of my own, but I had a life. It was now that I actually had nothing.

The hallway leading to the office looked so much smaller now. I still couldn't wrap my head around the fact that Max and Paige owned it.

She ushered me into the tiny office.

"You're all white, are you feeling okay?" Paige asked with eyes full of worry. "Here, sit down, I'm getting ice…" her words trailed off. "It's swelling really bad, Grey… what happened?"

I still couldn't answer her. She was looking down frowning like I was a little kid in trouble. My eyes burned and I used my good hand to shut them for a minute. I willed myself not to fucking cry. It wasn't the pain vibrating through my hand and up my arm, it was how she sliced my heart open. She needed me and I wasn't there. I had somehow let it all slip away. The most important thing I ever did in life was love her… and I failed.

I felt Paige's presence step closer to me and she hugged my head. I accepted it as an allowance to break down. I couldn't take it. Seeing her today and finding out that she didn't even remember what happened to us. She thought I'd broken up with her for all these years. It was too much. All the anger and hate I had built up and harbored for her over the past decade I now redirected to myself. I couldn't stop my thoughts. She thought I didn't care about her and then ended up pregnant. That was supposed to be my baby. Canyon was supposed to be my son.

I tried to calm myself down after I left her place. I really tried. But I couldn't take it. All of the anger and panic of what she had thought of me over the past decade slammed into me and I slammed my fist against my house. My brick house.

Served me right. I needed to be punished. I needed to feel pain. I should've tried harder back then. I should've ditched Texas and searched to face her. I had been so convinced that she was done with me, and I was a little pussy who wallowed in my self-pity instead of making sure she was okay.

"Uh.. am I interrupting?" I heard Max ask from the doorway.

Great. Now he'd see my cry too. I couldn't look up. Paige was one thing; Max was a different story.

"Babe, go take care of the front for a minute," Paige told him softly and she moved to close the door behind him.

Paige pulled up a chair across from mine. She pulled my hand into her lap and started cleaning it up and bandaging it silently. She poured a water bottle over it and then some hydrogen peroxide, making it sting like a motherfucker, but I deserved it. I willed myself not to flinch, but my whole body jerked as she tried to stretch my hand open.

"Well, that's not good," She paused for a beat. "This have anything to do with a tiny brunette and her little son?"

I took a deep breath and nodded.

"She doesn't remember it. Doesn't even think I was in it with her. She's telling the truth about it. She looked at my scar the other day and asked me about it. She had no idea."

Paige looked at me thoughtfully with confusion on her face.

"She thought I broke up with her. Like I would ever do that!"

She let my words absorb in.

"That does make sense," she finally said. "What happened to you guys was so sad. But…"

"But what?"

"That means she didn't dump you," Paige pointed out. "This whole time you thought she traded you in for that Kevin a-hole… she really didn't… isn't that kind of a good thing? He was like a rebound that went wrong."

"There's nothing good about this!" I boomed.

"Woah there, take it easy," Paige said soothingly. "I'm just trying to help you see the good."

I waved my mangled hand in front of her, "the good?!"

Paige rolled her eyes, "calm down, Romeo. Pause for a second and think about it. You boys never seem to be able to do that. Obviously you guys aired some things out today and that is definitely a good thing. There is like a decade of bad feelings that have festered between the two of you and they are just now all coming to the surface, it's probably going to be painful... but at least both of you are finding out truths that you need."

She blew out a breath, "But just because I'm feeling sorry for you does not mean I'm going to let you get away with not going to the hospital today. This is not cosmetic… your hand is not okay. It'll remain a blob or like fall off. You need a doctor. I'm going to get Max to take you now, okay?"

I nodded without looking at her and she stood to move and started shuffling out the door.

"Thanks, Mom," I told her.

She smirked at me and shook her head.

27 GREY – 13 YEARS AGO

I sped toward the corner, racing the defenseman. The puck was mine.

It was one of my last games with the Griffins and I needed to make it count.

I got there first, but was then slammed into the boards, his elbow against my head. He'd been doing that all game. I felt anger and adrenaline raging inside of me. He held me against the boards then, not letting up. Where was the whistle?

Next thing I knew, I wound up and slammed my glove against his helmet.

It moved fast then.

Our fist slamming into each other.

At some point my helmet fell off and I took one squarely to the face and felt the blood gush.

It just gave me more ammunition.

I usually wasn't a fighter. But this guy pushed me to it.

I felt one ref jerking me back by my jersey and another stood between us.

He got one good punch in but looking at him I knew I won the fight.

I smiled at him, which caused him to start chirping. I just blew him off and laughed, pussy.

I thought it was funny… until the ref was ushering me toward the door and not my team bench.

"What the fuck, he started it!" I protested, trying to yank my jersey from his grasp.

The ref just shook his head at me, "keep it up and I'll give you a game suspension as well."

I shook my head at the injustice. If he would've done his job I wouldn't have had to take matters into my own hands in the first place.

I looked back at the bench. I could hear Max's dad, our head coach, arguing on my behalf from all the way across the ice.

Walking down the hallway to our locked room, I took stalk of myself.

The front of my jersey was covered in blood. I wasn't in any pain yet because I was so pissed that I couldn't finish the last ten minutes of the game. I only felt a throbbing beginning from my nose as I opened the locker room door.

There were only two games left and everyone was fighting for some kind of commitment for next year. And here I was, sitting one of them out and losing opportunity. I shouldn't have let him get to me.

I kept the locker room light off. I wanted darkness; I was starting to feel a headache coming on.

Another concussion was not what I needed.

I threw my helmet at the wall and sat my ass down.

I tried some breathing exercises Jules had taught me but it really wasn't working. I was letting my temper get the best of me lately. I needed to check myself before it got worse. I couldn't afford many more head injuries. I had one bad concussion this season and I wanted to stay clear of anymore for the rest of my career.

I muttered a curse and started ripping my skate laces undone.

I heard a little knock on the locker room door then. Who would knock?

"Uh… yeah?" I called.

The door peeped open and I saw a fluttering of long light brown hair.

"Jules?" I asked incredulously. She wasn't supposed to be back here… but I guess the rest of the team was kind of busy at the moment.

She pulled the door all the way open then, and was immediately taken aback… it must've been the blood.

She flipped the lights on and took a couple strides toward me then and plopped herself next to me.

She touched my cheek and gave a sheepish grin. Her hand on my face made me feel better. She had a way of easing the trouble and anger stirring inside of me.

"Well, at least you won the fight?" She asked quietly.

I smirked at her and faltered. My nose started bleeding again.

She quickly got up and moved toward the tiny, partitioned bathroom and grabbed a wad of toilet paper.

"I can drive you to urgent care when you get all undressed?" She offered lightly as she tipped my head back slightly and kept a squeeze on the bridge of my nose.

"Fuck yeah, you can drive," I winked at her. I taught her this past year. We forged her grandparents' signatures on all her drivers ed stuff. If it were up to them, she'd never drive. For practice she had driven me to all the outdoor rinks in our vicinity. We had a good time.

She huffed, but the corner of her mouth twitched up like she was fighting a smile, "Focus, Grey. You might've broken it."

"No." My voice was muffled by the toilet paper now, but she heard me clearly.

She sighed.

"I'm just a bleeder. It looks worse than it is," I urged.

She gave me her signature "mom," look. Max called her Little Mama when she gave it to any of us.

"How am I supposed to let you go off and play wherever the hell you end up fully knowing you'll never go in if you're hurt?" She asked with a concerned look on her face. I could tell this really did bug her. "I'll be worried about you the whole time."

"Come with me," I grumbled. I was pissed off about the whole college thing. Her grandparents were making her go to their alma mater- probably the only college without a hockey team to their satisfaction. If they had one, I'd do anything to play there and be with her.

I reached up and touched the ends of her long hair. Even with her standing and me sitting I didn't have to reach too far up. I'd shot up past six foot this last year. She was destined to remain tiny forever. I liked the new height difference. It made me feel like I was her protector.

"Unless I'm ugly now and you won't have me anymore."

Her eyes danced as she laughed. "Stop talking babe, you're

making it worse… and a broken nose might help you round out the tough guy look that I find so sexy."

My girl. She always said the right thing and I loved her for it.

I couldn't help but think, as I grew rougher looking, she was growing more beautiful. This spring was her last season skating competitively and I was kind of relieved for her. She was still skating, but more so just for fun. She planned on skating up at college, but she already told the coach she wouldn't be competing. I'd never ever tell her what to do, but I fully backed her in that decision. Competing had become unhealthy for her, and without it she seemed to be growing healthier and more relaxed. You could clearly see that on her too. It seemed that as she backed off skating, she got boobs as a consolation. I was always very attracted to her but trading in her A-bra for a C one definitely was not a problem with me. She was pretty self-conscious about the change though. I had to make sure to let her know just how beautifully perfect she was… I was just giving them extra attention. I thanked God that I got her before the rest of the world got to see her.

"Love you," I said this in place of thank you all the time, and she knew it. A simple thank you wasn't enough for her.

She leaned down to kiss my forehead, "you're welcome and I love you very much, you bonehead, even though you smell very bad." I felt the corners of my lips curve up. "No laughing, it'll bleed!" She urged, which just made me want to more.

She grabbed a new wad of toilet paper and we sat there in silence for a couple moments. It felt like the bleeding had stopped. I closed my eyes hard against my headache.

Ever observant, Jules knew what to look for. She grabbed my chin and looked into my eyes with concern.

"Your head alright?" She knew me too well.

I nodded slowly and gave her wrist a tug to pull her into my lap. We sat there cuddled in comfort, my chin resting on her head.

"You still gonna love me if I lose all my teeth?" I mumbled.

Her tiny body shook with laughter.

"You didn't answer," I prodded, even though I was confident in her answer.

"You know I would, Greyson. I think I'm stuck with ya."

"Yupp."

The next few years would be tough, but we'd make it. She was the only girl for me in this world. She was my center, my home.

28 GREY – PRESENT

I pretty much cracked the knuckles on my right hand and my wrist.

I tried to leave, telling them I'd take care of it, but Max wouldn't let me. Probably on Paige's orders.

He slammed me back into the chair every time I started to get up. The doctors looked at us with unease.

A shy redheaded nurse came in and hooked me up to an IV and told me it'd relax me.

Max winked at her. I doubted there was just IV in that bag, but I signed shit and didn't even know what it was for.

And now because of Max, after wasting the whole day there, I was leaving the place with a bulky, stupid-ass cast from my forearm to my fingers to hold them in place.

"I could've fucking taped it up every day. Not my first time punching a wall," I grunted.

Max scrunched his eyebrows in concern and hit the parking garage's elevator button, "Me neither but I've never punched a brick wall as hard as I could. You couldn't walk like a couple paces inside and choose drywall? Big difference there, bud."

We stood in silence until the elevator released us. I was still pissed, not at him, but at myself and the whole situation.

"Only motherfucking girls get casts," I spat at Max as I continued to follow him through the garage to his car.

Max looked at me and cocked an eyebrow, "Dude, that is one of the dumbest things I've ever heard you say, and you've said a lot of dumb shit. Did you not hear the doctor? They're looking at it again in a couple weeks and you might need surgery. You don't want to mess with knuckles and shit," he warned. "Don't you ever wanna play pass with the kids again? A hand is kind of important."

"What fucking kids?" I snapped at him before I could register what he was saying. For the first time I regretted what I'd done. Not for myself, but for my team. For Canyon.

"Jesus, don't bite my head off, I'm just saying."

He unlocked his car, and I quickly threw the door open and slammed my ass into the seat.

Smitty was already sprawled out playing video games on the sofa when Max and I entered my place.

"Make yourself at home," I mumbled.

He looked at me then, taking in the cast, "Yikes bro, tough break."

I ignored him and proceeded to my kitchen. I needed a beer.

"Woah there, bud. Not today, you've had a ton of shit already pumped into you," Max chided me like I was a child and swiped the beer I'd just placed on the counter. He popped the top off and took a swig for himself.

"You're welcome for taking you in," he said and turned towards my living room to join Smitty.

Smitty looked at me like he was bracing for impact.

"Wanna play?" He grimaced.

I looked at him dryly.

"Sure, let me just break this off with a hammer first."

"Sleep it off. You've got practice tomorrow morning with the kiddies," Max said.

Great. No way I could face her now. I'd have to hide my hand from her out of pure embarrassment.

29 JULES PRESENT

When it came to morning practices, I was probably in the minority of athletes, but I always loved them. Waking up fresh and feeling so powerful being the first to mark up the clean ice was an unbeatable feeling.

I was happy Canyon was getting to experience it.

I hoped he loved them as much as I had. I selfishly planned on trying to foster a little love of them in him by restarting a tradition of mine this Saturday. I was going to take him to the Tim Horton's across the street for some donuts after finishing up here at the rink.

The other unbeatable feeling that came with morning practices- leaving the rink at 8 or 9am with a weird feeling in your limbs from leaving the cold rink and going into warmer weather, and already having accomplished so much in the day- that definitely deserved a celebratory donut. Grey used to feel the same way.

I was finding it was just as fun to do the morning run as a parent and experiencing it again through his little eyes.

I marched up the bleachers to my usual spot and wrapped my Griffins blankets around myself before taking my seat on the metal bleachers.

I sipped my coffee and waved to a couple other moms dotting the bleachers.

I was already a fan of this team. It seemed like everyone was enjoying their own little peace and they were only interested in their own kid. I'd been around the rink long enough to know that in a month or two the screamer or obnoxious bragger or ice time complainer would come through the woodworks. I would enjoy the peace for now though.

As soon as the zam left the ice, the rink's peaceful hum was the only sound that could be heard.

Our little guys finally started to appear through the locker room doors. A couple rugrats were struggling to open the door.

Smitty bobbled over to them, play shoving them out of the way, and got the job done.

I had to smile to myself. It was really unbelievable that these troublemakers, the ones who were once written up by rink management for running a locker boxing tournament complete with a by-in and winning jackpot, were the ones running a team of little kids.

Canyon zoomed onto the ice then, being chased by Troy. I wondered if Canyon would become a little troublemaker one day. He was so innocent right now, my little angel. I supposed that all troublemaker's moms thought their children were angels as well though.

Greyson, the last to exit the locker room, dumped a bucket of pucks onto the ice, and stepped out, closing the rink's door behind him.

It became pretty clear that Grey had taken the head coach role and Smitty fell into assisting.

Grey took command of the practices. He'd have all the boys kneeling in front of him talking, while Smitty would demonstrate what he was saying to do.

After watching Canyon's turn at running a drill, I found my eyes glued to Grey.

I noticed he looked curious and a bit awkward holding his stick only with his left hand. I'd watched enough games to pretty much memorize his stance, stride, and shot. I could pick him out of a lineup any day. He was 100% a righty.

A couple drills later he bent down to pick up a water bottle and had to drop the stick from his left hand in order to do it.

He was definitely babying his right side.

"How goes it, girly?"

I jumped.

I was so focused on watching I didn't notice Paige approach, which was stupid of me- I knew better than to be ignorant of my surroundings. On the other hand, it felt like the rink was healing me, allowing me to feel so comfortable that I wasn't as worried anymore.

"Good morning," I smiled. Friendship with Paige had always come so easily.

"Mind if I sip some morning coffee with you?" She smiled brightly and pushed her Beanie out of her eyes.

"I would love the company," I scootched over so she could have some of my blanket.

"Wow, this feels like old times," she laughed. "But now our guys are old geezers."

I grimaced. Greyson wasn't mine. Not by a long shot. I hadn't been as lucky to have my first love work out.

She obviously didn't realize her mistake, or didn't think it was a mistake, and she kept talking.

"Hey, remember when the old rink manager Craig made 'Wanted dead or alive' signs of the boys?" She cackled. The memory made me chuckle as well. Their roughhousing and stealing of beers from Benny's would get out of hand. I felt bad for Craig a lot of times growing up.

"Poor Craig," I mused, smoothing out the blanket on my lap.

Paige shook her head in agreement.

"So, what number's your little babe?" she asked.

"Right there along the boards in line for the next drill, with the blue penny- he's number 77."

Canyon and Troy chose that moment to brawl with each other and fall to the ice.

Paige got a kick out of it, "Well, looks like history might be repeating here."

Max made an appearance then. He always looked wrinkled and scruffy. He walked along the side of the boards and made his way into the team box. He ushered Grey over.

"Is something wrong with Grey's right side?" I didn't want it to seem like I cared, but I wanted to know.

"What makes you think that?" her eyebrows shot up, totally giving away that she did know something.

"Uh.. never mind." I didn't want to come off like I'd been watching him, even though I had. The whole kitchen argument was still fresh in my mind and I didn't want to unpack it all just yet. He was Canyon's coach, and friend now apparently, and I didn't want to complicate the now with the past.

"You're right though, there is something wrong. Those boys have a hard time managing their emotions, I swear," She rolled her eyes.

I snapped my neck back towards her, "Huh?"

She balked at me, "Girl! He left your place torn up the other day, couldn't you tell?" She held her hands up to say she was innocent. "I'm not blaming anyone. No one's fault. The stars' fault maybe," she said curiously. "You guys are star-crossed lovers if I've ever seen a pair."

She shook her head. I still didn't understand what she was saying.

"Paige… what?"

She sighed and turned to face me and put her hands on my shoulders. She smudged her glossy lips together.

"Both of you are so dumb- no offense- when it comes to each other. He gave himself a panic attack after leaving your place because he was so upset over how you thought he had dumped you and left you alone for all these years. He had it in his head that you were the bad guy who dumped him. So he had all this resentment towards you for years and he just then realized it was misplaced. He was so angry and panicked that he proceeded to punch his brick house and shatter his hand."

She raised her eyebrows at me.

"And then he came to me crying thinking I could fix his little broken wing because of his hospital scaries- but that part's kind of cute actually in his sad puppy dog kinda way that he gets, ya know?"

I was stunned.

I felt my jaw drop. He really did think that I had dumped him…?

I replayed her entire rant in my head.

Then a giggle erupted.

I clamped my hand over my mouth.

But then Paige laughed too.

We were both losing it.

"This is so mean; we have to stop!" I said, wiping the tears from my eyes and holding my stomach.

"You're going to make me pee, girl!" Paige struggled to say between laughs.

I took some deep breaths and calmed myself down.

"I am the worst. Please don't say I laughed at him about this. It's actually really sweet in a messed-up way. I am not laughing at him hurting himself, I just lost it because I know exactly the kind of sad puppy-look he gets," I explained. "Like what were you going to do with a broken hand?! Remember when he had me butterfly his one eyebrow together because he wouldn't go in? There's still a hole there! It's been like over ten years!"

"Girl, you do not have to explain to me, and I totally know," she said, shaking her head.

"Jesus, that's the first time I've laughed like that in a long time," I told her, trying to make sure no black smudges were left on my face from runny mascara.

She patted me on the knee, "never leave me again, girl."

Grey was still talking to Max over by the team box, so I could really look at him. Now that she's said it, his right hockey glove did look weird, like it wasn't on all the way.

"Is it a bad break?" I asked her, internally cringing and wishing I could give him a hug.

She shrugged, "if he does what the doctor says it'll heal up fine, but if he moves it, like breaking the cast with a hammer as he threatened, then he'll probably need surgery."

"Jeez," I paused then. "So, he really didn't dump me?" I mulled over this question all night. The breakup texts were there on my phone.

"Jules," she looked at me sternly. "He did not dump you. He was a wreck. I think he's been a wreck ever since that summer. Hockey was his anger outlet. The real and raw emotions he's shown over the last couple weeks have been more than he's shown in the past decade."

I didn't know how to feel about that information. Shock that a strange miscommunication seemed to stray both of our fates away from each other. And sadness, that he'd felt so empty the past nine years. He was such a happy guy, always the one to look on the bright side of things. I knew in my heart that if he had felt the same way after the breakup as I had, he had the worse end of it because Canyon had brightened my life.

"I still feel like I'm missing something," I told her. "We were in that accident together?"

Paige grimaced, "Yes, 100%. That's how he got that scar, Jules," she traced a finger down her jawline where Grey's skin was affected.

"Girl," Paige looked at me seriously, "that boy would still walk through fire for you."

I turned my attention back to the ice. That was a lot to take in.

Could it be true? All these years I told myself that part of my life was done. He had thrown away what we had. I held a grudge against him because I still couldn't look at other guys. I compared everyone to him and how I felt with him, and no one could ever match up to that. A lot of times I wondered if the passing of time and the way Kevin treated me had just made me romanticize what I had with Greyson; That I had put him on some kind of misplaced pedestal in my mind and the love we shared had actually just been all me and one-sided. But sifting through my memories, I knew that wasn't true. He had wanted and loved me too.

I caught his eye then. He was looking up in the stands directly at me. There was no guessing about it. Neither of us showed emotion. We just studied each other in the new light.

30 JULES - PRESENT

"Hey bud, great work out there!" I tousled my son's sweaty hair as he walked up to me struggling under the weight of his bag.

"Thanks, my shot's gettin better, right?" He asked hopefully.

"100 percent better," I assured him. "I have a surprise destination in mind though so let's get out of here. You sure you don't want me to take your bag?" I asked him.

He smirked up at me, "no way, Mom. And I'm almost as big as you anyways."

"Ha!" I exclaimed. I had about three to four more years of being taller than him. "Not by a long shot, kid," I joked. "Let's go."

Canyon's eyes lit up at the sight of the fresh donuts. He got two sprinkled and some chocolate milk, claiming he was a growing boy, and I got a crawler and a vanilla iced coffee, my all-time favorites.

At the table, Canyon happily munched on his donuts and relayed everything from practice.

"So what was up with Coach Grey's hand?" I asked him.

"Ohh, Coach Smitty said he got in a fight with a wall!" He exclaimed like it was the craziest thing he'd heard in his eight years.

"Yikes, you better not go all psycho on my walls," I told him.

Canyon shook his head in disbelief and shoved some more donut in his mouth.

Right then, the door chimed welcoming a new customer. I looked up and was surprised to see Grey.

But he had, after all, been part of the crew that would steal away from the rink for donuts between morning practices. In the back of my mind, I had been wondering if he remembered the tradition; the fact that he did punched me with a bittersweet nostalgia.

He looked comfortable wearing a light grey sweatshirt with the hood pulled up and soft, baggy sweatpants, and Nike sliders. I stifled a laugh at the idea that he still dressed like a 17-year-old boy.

His face faltered when he saw us, which caused a wave of disappointment I wish I could've ignored, and he noticeably moved quick to tuck his right hand into his hoody pocket.

He nodded with a tight-lipped smile and then walked briskly up to the counter with his long and steady strides.

Canyon had been studying him the whole time as well.

"Think he has anyone to eat with?" He asked me with concerned little eyes.

I was unsure of what to say to that, so I answered truthfully, "I really don't know, babe." After all, he could've been meeting people here.

He craned his neck to see Grey.

My sweet boy. Gratitude and sadness hit me at the same time. I was thankful for my little partner in crime, but sad for Grey. He seemingly had no one.

"Thank you for being my donut buddy," I patted my boy's cheek.

A minute later Grey emerged carrying a tray with his left hand. He walked to the farthest corner of the diner from us and sat by himself, keeping his head down and his shoulders hunched up. The sunshine from the windows glowed on him. He had to be hot sitting there, but knowing him he was probably too embarrassed to switch seats. I internally laughed at that notion. Personality couldn't change that much in a decade, could it? I really could still read him.

Before even realizing it, Canyon had popped off his chair and was running towards him.

I sat there sipping my coffee watching as my son was gesturing over to me.

Grey looked my way and made eye contact with me looking unsure of what to do. This was totally the puppy dog look Paige had referenced. It really did make me want to give him a hug and say that everything would be okay. But maybe that was the mom in me coming out as well.

I gave him a slight smile and nodded and that was all the assurance he needed. He stood slowly, towering over Canyon, and let him lead the way.

We had to hash out what had happened all those years ago, but today I just wanted to enjoy his company and live in our old tradition with my son.

Canyon noisily pulled a chair over for him from the table next to us.

"Good morning," I told him.

"Uh, hullo," he said. "Still can't have morning practice without a donut after, eh?" He joked lightly and gave a hesitant smile. I felt a painful twinge in my heart. A mixture of sorrow and hurt knowing that I had used to kiss that same smile… but I had to stop thinking of him that way. He was Canyon's coach and friend now, I repeated to myself for the hundredth time.

"I'm on my second!" Canyon said, earning a laugh from Grey.

"And I see you still think donuts are only dessert?" I asked him, gesturing to his bagel.

"Bor-ing," Canyon chirped, shaking his head at him.

"It's way too heavy to start the day with," he countered, relaxing a bit. "At least he's got the chocolate milk right," he ruffled Canyon's hair. "A hockey guy's favorite."

"I thought beer was?" Canyon asked.

"Canyon!" I warned.

Grey big shoulders shook as he laughed.

His 6'4 frame was so much larger than Canyon's and mine. It seemed funny that he was the one with the extra chair.

"You taught him right," he said softly with an amused quirk of his lip.

I shook my head and took a bite of my donut.

He started to take the knife with his left hand and stopped.

Canyon and I were both watching him then, probably making him feel awkward. He had yet to take his right hand out of his hoodie pocket.

"Something wrong?" I asked him, teasing him a bit. I knew I should've kept eating and not brought attention to it, but I couldn't help it.

He looked sheepishly at me and shook his head no. He

proceeded to try to turn the bagel sideways and stab the knife through it. It was not going his way.

"Fuck it," he growled under his breath and took a bite out of the bagel unsliced and without his beloved butter, something I knew he hated to do.

"Oooh, potty word," Canyon looked at me questioningly, wondering if I was going to get mad.

Greys cheeks turned red. A rare sight. I hadn't seen him so unsure of himself since the first time he asked to kiss me at sixteen. It was endearing and saddening at the same time.

"Here," I grabbed the bagel from his large, rough hand and the butter from in front of him and helped the guy out.

"Thanks," he said quietly. "Sorry for the… um, curse."

I rolled my eyes, "the kid knows them all, also knows not to say them aloud, right?"

Kevin had a sailor's mouth. One of Canyon's first words was shit.

"Right!" Canyon said. He laid a little hand on Grey's muscular shoulder and cocked his head to the side, "So Coach, what was it like playing for the Caps? Me and mom watched a ton of your games, but the Caps were our favorites. We think you played best there. We went once!"

I inwardly groaned. Him knowing we followed his career made me feel self-conscious, but Grey's face lit up like hearing that made his day. I never brought him up to Canyon, but once he found out for himself that Grey played at the League as a kid, he was automatically his favorite athlete. I think Canyon had put two and two together, realizing that I had skated at the League around the same time as him. But he never guessed at the nature of our relationship and that was fine with me. I think watching Grey play in the NHL gave him a little hope that the dream could actually be real, and I think subconsciously I had allowed Grey to be part of our dream because maybe he had always been part of mine.

"Yeah? You went to a game?" He asked Canyon and turned to look at me. It was my turn to blush in embarrassment.

"It was a fun trip," I shrugged. I was too self-conscious to look at him in the eye. It would be too telling. I looked away and flinched at the second part of the memory.

We had passed through DC with Kevin on a business trip. Kevin left us at the hotel pretty much the entire weekend, so I figured I'd take Canyon to a game, knowing in the back of my mind that Grey would be on the ice. It started a hell of an argument between Kevin and I, but it was worth it in my mind to give Canyon a fun experience.

"Man, it was great. We sat way high up, but it was a really good game. You got two goals. We went skating at the statue garden place too that trip. It was my birthday. I would skate there all the time if I lived there," Canyon shook his head seriously. My little son had an incredible memory, and usually I was very proud of it… just not at this moment.

"The statue garden, eh?" Grey looked at me while continuing conversation with Canyon. "Your mom always did love a good outdoor rink." He winked at me.

It surprised me that he remembered that detail and it caused a ping of sorrow to hit my stomach. We had gone to so many together. That was how he taught me to drive. How could it be that this man was part of so much of my life?

"Oh, she still does, right Mom? When we go to tournaments in other cities, we always try to find an outdoor rink. It's our thing, Coach. Oh man! Wait! You'll see now! We goin any good places this season?" Canyon's words sped up as he got more excited.

I shifted a little uncomfortably. I felt exposed by my little son. I did call it "our thing," but it was something I always done with Grey before Canyon. I was afraid he'd turn cold at hearing that, but when I sneaked a look at Grey, he looked… excited.

Right then Canyon knocked over the remainder of his chocolate milk when he was gesturing with his hands.

I moved quickly to fix up the spill with the napkins we had. Canyon sucked in a breath and ran to get more napkins, calling out a "Sorry Mom!"

I followed my son with my eyes, not wanting him to stray too far. When I looked back down at the chocolate mess, I noticed some had spilled on Grey.

"Ohmygod, I'm so sorry!" I told him.

He just shook his head and laughed, "totally fine, Juju."

His use of my old nickname caused me to stop and look up at him.

"I'm so happy you still do that," he said in a low voice.

His voice caused something in me to stir. I told myself it was just old love. But I felt justified in a way. He would not have remembered that detail if our entire love story was a sham…. He didn't have to explain what he meant with those words. He was talking about my need to search out outdoor rinks. After I learned to drive, it became my favorite thing to do in cities. I did it on every competition weekend I ever went away for and every tournament I ever went to watch Grey in. As soon as Canyon turned two, I had him on the ice so that he could join me every time we went on a business trip with Kevin. I wanted to share the hidden gem of fun with my son. Kevin never appreciated the beauty and fun of an outdoor rink.

As soon as Canyon was back and the milky mess was cleaned up, we fell into comfortable hockey conversation.

Canyon clearly saw him as larger than life, wanting to know all the inside information on the NHL, and he seemed to want to know just as much about Canyon.

Grey started to loosen up and eventually took his hand out of his hoodie pocket and laid it on the table.

It was no wonder he kept it tucked away, it wouldn't have been any use. The black cast held his first three fingers in place, so that only his pinky and thumb peaked out.

My heart broke a little knowing that he had beaten himself up over our conversation.

But I also felt a fluttering of hope, which was bad. I told myself I needed to shut it down. Too much had happened between us to go back to what was. I couldn't confuse the possibility of friendship with something more.

Grey caught me looking at his hand and it seemed he was holding his breath waiting for my reaction.

"Does it hurt?" Canyon asked, breaking the ice.

He paused for a beat, not taking his eyes off mine.

"Other things hurt worse," he said softly, causing the fluttering sensation again.

"Like when that Detroit player shoved you into their team box?" Canyon asked while launching his little body at an unsuspecting Grey in a mock check.

Grey almost flew out of his chair, "I'm on the injured list!" He called out while trying to regain his balance.

"That's it," Grey said, standing and grabbing up Canyon and flinging him over his shoulder, "Two minutes for charging!"

Taking in the whole scene, I couldn't stop laughing. Really laughing for the second time today. I decided then that it was a good thing to have these friends back in our lives.

When we finished, Grey walked us out of the diner and to my car.

Canyon quickly crawled into the backseat leaving us to awkwardly face each other. I put my sunglasses on to shield my eyes.

"Jules," he pulled his hood off and gave me a pleading look. "Can we talk?"

I could see the boy I knew in him at that moment. It would be so easy to just hug him like I used to. To kiss his chest and look up at him, into his dark eyes guarded by the longest eyelashes I'd ever seen. I imagined it would feel so natural, like coming home. He was so large and secure. I fought my desire to do it. I still had questions that stopped me. I couldn't forget how broken I'd been when he left me. I could never allow myself to be that vulnerable or weak again.

I had Canyon to worry about. He was my first priority now.

But that didn't stop me from saying, "Yes."

Relief washed over his tough face.

"Want to come over for pizza? I have a pool. Canyon can play with Smitty and Max?" His eyebrows drew together in question.

My heart beat faster. To see his house and talk with just him… it was something I'd wanted for so long.

"Pool?" I tried to make the words come out normal, but my throat felt tight with anticipation. "Could Canyon bring Troy?"

He smiled then, "Perfect."

"Want to text me the address and time?" I asked.

He looked at me in indecision then and grimaced. He rubbed the stubble on his chin with his hand.

"Wait here," he said. He turned and walked back into the diner.

A minute later he reappeared with a napkin that read an address in the handwriting I had long ago memorized: "welcome anytime, but 4 would be perfect."

I looked at him strangely.

"I'm seriously never texting you any important information ever again," he said lightly, but his eyes looked serious. He gave me a wink and turned on his heel to walk to his wrangler.

31 JULES – 3 YEARS AGO

It was Canyon's sixth birthday and the two of us were cooped up in this damn hotel room. I breathed deeply and closed my eyes against the rising sun's light coming in through the shades of the huge suite. We'd already been here three full days. When Kevin suggested we come with him on this business trip I agreed because I thought he wanted to be with his son on his birthday. How pathetic of me for believing that. He was a twisted son of a bitch. I knew he didn't care about me. But now he was treating Canyon with disdain as well.

This was probably the first birthday he would remember and damn it all if it wasn't a good memory.

It was decided. I would make it a great day. We were leaving this damn hotel.

He was laying in the hotel bed next to me and I lightly ran my nails through his hair like he loved. His angelic little face dotted with freckles was just coming out of sleep. I loved this little boy more than I'd ever loved anyone. Even more than him… but I would not say his name.

Tonight, I would take Canyon to a Caps game. He loved hockey. He knew practically all the big players and their stats. It was amazing to me how much his little brain remembered. Maybe I could even get a Happy Birthday message written to him on the big screen.

I would just have to swallow my pride over the fact that the boy

I previously loved with my whole life would be on the ice in front of us.

I pushed down anxiety over being in the same building as him. He would never know. He would never care. It was an admission I had learned to accept. Maybe I could block out all the hate and regret and just remember the good for tonight. There had been a lot of good.

He stirred awake then, "Morning, Mommy." He smiled with his eyes still closed and I leaned down to kiss his little nose.

"I have a big birthday surprise for you today," I told him sweetly. "Happy birthday my perfect little boy." I moved to get up, but he took my hand and put it back on his head. He wanted me to continue racking his hair. I couldn't help but give in to his cute request. One day he wouldn't want it anymore and he was my only baby. I reached over to grab the clicker with my free hand to change the station to a cartoon and then grabbed my coffee.

I was almost afraid Canyon was going to fall asleep during the game tonight, but he had a cherry icee, candy, and popcorn in front of him, so I bet that would probably keep him wired.

"This is the best, Mom! Thank you!" He said.

I patted his cheek and stole some of his candy, "No problem, baby. So, who's going to win?"

He rattled off some stats of the guys on Capitals and their opponents tonight, the Boston Bruins.

"I really like Ericksen, but Greyson Scott is my favorite player," he said. I almost choked on the popcorn.

"Gr-... Greyson Scott?" I asked him. I couldn't believe I'd said his name aloud to my child. It felt like a dirty secret for some reason. Probably because I'd loved him and not his father.

"Yeah, mom. He lived in Northfield. Just like me!" he said.

I nodded.

It was almost like him mentioning his name allowed me to look for him on the ice.

I immediately picked him out. I still knew his skating. I secretly sometimes did turn a specific game on to see him. But I hadn't known my son liked watching him as well.

"He's on fire right now, scoring up a storm lately. Maybe he'll score for my birthday, you think?" he turned to me with a hopeful look.

I smiled at him and ruffled his hair. I loved his innocence, "Maybe he will," I told him.

Grey was on the starting line, front and center. He took his face-off stance the exact same way he had as a high school kid. He was just much larger now. The camera zoomed in on his face and I had to swallow down self-pity. He was still such a beautiful guy. But his eyes did not look playful anymore. They looked hard and cold. I hoped that was just his game face. He had been a good boy, and a good guy. I silently prayed the world hadn't turned him into a bad man.

As soon as the game started, my little man was moving around in his seat as he watched the game, and I couldn't help but feel joy. I was so happy I stole away and took him to this game.

With Canyon cheering next to me, it was almost impossible to not get into the game. I soon found myself cheering and high-fiving my son over the Caps triumphs.

But I couldn't help but think of the irony. Of him down there living out his dream and me sitting up here looking down at him from the nose-bleeds.

Canyon fell asleep on the Metro, and again in the Uber. He usually didn't stay up past his bedtime at 9pm and it was already almost midnight. I was thankful he was still small enough that I could carry him inside.

He stood up by himself in the elevator and rested his little head against my stomach. I closed my eyes hard, cherishing this last minute of peace with him before we had to answer to Kevin.

"Fucking hell," Kevin mouthed at me, shaking his head as soon as I opened the door. I was hit with a massive stench of alcohol.

I held Canyon's ear against my stomach as we shuffled into the room, pushing past him.

I laid Canyon in bed and took off his shoes slowly. He immediately curled into a ball and pulled the covers higher onto himself.

I cherished how peaceful he looked.

A second later a heavy hand gripped my upper arm and ripped me forward so hard I almost fell on my face.

I hoped he was pushing me into the hallway. He couldn't do

anything then.

But I was wrong. He shoved me into the privacy of the small bathroom.

As soon as the door closed behind us, I turned to face him and was met with a splintering slap across the face.

I held my face and willed the tears not to come forward. That would only give him more power and show him that what he did had worked.

I stayed silent. I knew the drill. He was drunk off his ass. It showed in his red face and crazed eyes.

"What the fuck, Julianna," he whispered. "Where the fuck were you two?"

"I took him out for his birthday," I said boldly.

"Where?" he demanded.

I paused. I didn't want to let him know. Because he would twist the reason why I had gone.

"Where?" he demanded harsher and took a step closer to me. I commanded myself not to flinch as he neared.

"Where!" he shouted this time and I did flinch.

"A hockey game," I told him.

He seemed to back off then.

But I was wrong.

I felt another heavy hand hit my face and this time the force almost made me fall into the tub.

"It's going to show!" I hissed. I tried to hide the hysteria I was feeling.

That finally caused him to back off.

But he wasn't done taking shots. He gave a snide laugh, "Went to watch the old boyfriend, huh?" he spit. "He doesn't want you. Ungrateful," he spit.

I hadn't realized I was holding my breath until he left the bathroom and I finally exhaled.

I tried to calm my breathing and think back to how worth it going to the game had been.

I thought of my precious boy's smile and willed myself not to cry. My throat burned. We had to get out of this. There had to be a way out. I had messed up. But I didn't deserve this. No one did.

32 GREY - PRESENT

I stood in front of the grill alternating between sipping my beer and moving the hot dogs and hamburgers around with my left hand. I couldn't stop moving. A nervous energy had come over me ever since she said yes a few hours ago.

Paige, Max, Smitty, and Ashlie were all chatting on the patio, but I couldn't hear them over my thoughts.

I'd been waiting for this talk for so long, and apparently, she had too.

Having breakfast with her and Canyon earlier had almost been a dream come true. The sadness that came over her when she saw my hand wrecked me, reminding me of how messed up everything between us had become. But it also showed me that she still cared for me.

I wasn't sure where her head was at, but I still wanted everything with her. So bad. I wanted the weird wall between us to be decimated. I wanted to be able to touch her and hold her. I wanted to be the one to take care of her and Canyon. I wanted to let her know that I knew she was strong and capable, but she shouldn't have had to do it all on her own. Neither of us ever wanted to be away from each other. I could see that clearly now. With some twisted f'ed up cut off from both sides we had been isolated from each other.

Even if she didn't want me in the way I wanted her, I'd take whatever she'd give me, even if that meant just friendship and being a coach to Canyon. I just knew that I'd never leave her again. I owed it to her. She was mine to protect all those years ago and I failed.

I'd lived so cynically and had just gone through the motions for so long, she was like a lifeline back to who I was. I just hoped she could see that we could still have what was ours- the life that was meant for us.

Neither of us were the same anymore; life changed us as it changes everyone, but I was still so drawn to her, even more so than before, if that were possible. She was stronger now, anyone who knew her could tell that. Watching her with Canyon was equal parts joyous and painful because it was exactly how I'd always pictured her as a mom. It gave me relief that she'd had him these past eight years. I'd had no one. I'd been stuck in a living hell without any sort of relationships or love. It was just now, since I'd been back here that I realized how much I'd missed in the past years.

"Hey," Paige came up from behind me, "she just texted me she'll be here in a minute. Why don't you go inside and greet them, Smitty can take over the grill."

My mouth went dry. This would be it. This conversation would decide if we could get back on track after all these years. I took another sip of beer.

Paige patted my shoulder, "Relax! It's Jules. She came home to us. Go get you girl," she whispered and gave me a wink.

I nodded and nervously moved toward my front door to wait for them.

I could see Canyon and Troy already running for my door in swim trunks and with their goggles already on. They both had a wadded-up beach towel under their little arms.

Jules was still at her car pulling out a beach bag.

I flung the door open wide so that they didn't have to knock and held out my fist for a knuckle punch.

"Mom said you have a pool?!" Canyon asked for confirmation.

"Yupp, straight through the house to the backyard. I have an important job for you two though, c'mere."

They looked at each other in question and then followed me over to my living room closet.

I took two superjet water guns out and handed them to the boys.

They looked at me in awe and cheered.

"Now, here's the challenge," I told them seriously. "You want to soak the shi- wups- crap out of Max an Smitty, but you don't want to get the ladies. Ladies get real mad when you mess up their hair and makeup, make sure you remember that," I told them.

They both nodded vigorously and were practically jumping out of their skin with excitement.

"Go get 'em, boys!" I yelled as they scampered off. I looked up to see Jules enter through the door then.

She looked effortlessly beautiful, with her hair piled up in a messy bun, a t-shirt that said hockey mom, cut-off shorts that showed off her toned and impossibly long legs for such a short girl, and some white vans tennis shoes.

"Wow, you're already stirring up trouble, aren't you, Mr. Scott?" Jules asked me with a smirk.

I was about to say something smartass back, but I noticed the container she was carrying.

"No way!"

She laughed and her face turned a cute shade of pink, "missed my brownies?"

"Oh my God. Can I have one right now? These are all mine right?"

She giggled as I took the container from her and easily lifted the beach bag off her shoulder and transferred it to mine. Her brownies were like crack to me as a teen. Loved them.

I ripped open the container and shoved a whole one in my mouth.

"Damn" I said with closed eyes, savoring it. Realizing what a weird ass I was being, I flashed my eyes open to look at her, but her eyes just twinkled with amusement.

"You have a beautiful house," she said, craning her neck to look around a bit.

The word beautiful was meant for her. But I didn't want to say it and scare her away. We were on shaky ground, and I didn't know where I stood with her. The look she'd given me in her kitchen was still burned into my mind.

So instead, I cleared my throat and asked, "Want a tour?"

She nodded shyly.

I set her stuff down and reached for her hand. Unnecessary, but I needed to touch her. Just holding her hand made me feel like a fricken teenager. My heart was beating faster from the combination of nerves and hope.

I led her through my kitchen, which was still pretty empty, but I was a fan of the exposed brick.

I had only been here a couple of weeks and this was the first time I was actually settling down in a place. I wanted to get it right; to make it feel like home. I was kind of anxious to show her because I stupidly had this hope that she'd like it here.

I led her downstairs, which I had recently started working on. I framed some of my old jerseys and set it up to look like a mini movie theater complete with a dozen recliners and a huge screen. I topped it off with a pool table and air hockey table in the corners of the room.

She looked around with wide eyes, "Wow, this looks great. Canyon is going to be super jealous." Her voice was laced with awe and I couldn't help but feel a little proud at my homemaking skills.

"He'll approve? I was thinking of having the whole team over before I have to cover the pool for the season."

She nodded, "They would love that." She looked back at me and patted my chest, my stomach really because she was so short with flat shoes on, "Look at you, just like a Chip Gaines," she joked, and her eyes crinkled in the corners. The exact smile I was used to looking at as a teen. She seemed less unsure of herself now; she possessed a more mature beauty, and damn… I think I was even more attracted to her.

When she moved towards the first jersey on the wall my heart practically stopped.

The Texas Titans. I immediately wished I'd covered that one up. It was agonizing to see her looking at it. That jersey was worn when I couldn't control my emotions over losing her. I'd been devastated all season. It still held such raw emotion because she was supposed to be there. Watching her looking at it made me feel like I was going through a time warp and losing my footing. I rubbed a hand over my face.

"Here, let's go upstairs."

She turned from the frame and smiled at me, her eyes looking glossy.

I turned away from her before I lost it. I was afraid of what she'd say.

"I'm so proud of you," I heard her say quietly.

I felt my chest swell a little in consolation.

I'd never really felt anything about my accomplishments past the celebration of a goal in the moment, but hearing her say it made me feel genuinely proud of my career for possibly the first time.

I turned back around and reached for her hand and caught her eye for a brief second. There were no reservations there. But those unshed tears in her eyes gutted me.

We made our way to the second floor in shared silence. The house had an open floor plan and a ton of windows; you could see the entire kitchen and living room and outside to the pool from where we stood in the upstairs hallway. She peeked around taking it all in, and her eyes rested on the pool outside.

You could hear the boys' rambunctious laughter all the way from here.

Smitty grabbed Canyon and was jumping into the pool with him.

Her eyes danced with laughter.

"Always the jokester, right?"

"Smitty or my son?" She countered. I didn't know Canyon well enough yet to know if he was a jokester like Smitty, but I wanted to. I planned on trying my hardest to find out.

I tugged her towards the three guest rooms then.

After looking through them, I turned to head back downstairs. She paused behind me.

"What about your room?" She hugged herself as she said it. "Your place is a bit chilly, just FYI."

I looked down at her tiny self on the edge of shivering and I felt laughter bubbling up inside of me.

She looked at me confusedly.

I took a couple steps down the stairs and turned to look into her eyes which were level with mine then. I shrugged, "I used to keep the windows open on purpose so that you'd want me as a blanket. Did you know that?"

Her jaw dropped then, and she swatted me on the chest. "You are not serious."

It was such brief contact, but I wanted her to keep touching me.

I took steps up to tower over her tiny frame, "Dead," I told her, raising my eyebrows. "But my room… I didn't clean up…"

She placed her small hand in the middle of my chest and smiled up at me. I wondered if she could tell just how fast it was pumping.

"Wow," she laughed. "You sound just like Canyon right now. But you really think I don't know that? Funny, Greyson Scott. You could barely see your bed because it was covered in dirty clothes half the time in college. I remember sleeping in your bed and finding random socks. I want to see it," she said confidently. Her eyes twinkled with laugher.

Of course I perked up at her even mentioning the word bed to me like I was sixteen again.

"Well, you asked for it," I opened the door then and she squeezed past me. Her hair still smelled like lavender and that knowledge made me weak.

She stood in the center of the room. I tried to see it from her eyes.

A pile of dirty clothes, an unmade bed with waded up sheets in the corner, and nothing on the walls except the one frame I didn't hang in the basement: my Griffins jersey.

She walked over to it and touched the edge.

A small candid picture was in the corner of the frame. Max kissing Paige, Ashlie and Smitty smiling, and Jules sitting on my lap, touching my shitty, patchy 18-year-old beard.

It had dust on it, because I never dared to touch it or take it off that frame. It was given to me after I signed with Brecklin. She was there when I received it and she was the one to add that picture to the corner.

I always kept it in my room. I wasn't sure if it was a good thing or not. Half the time it felt like I was just torturing myself by having it there- showing everything I'd lost. But the other half of the time, I felt at peace at least knowing those people, the ones that mattered the most to me, were somewhere out there in the world living and breathing and struggling just like I was.

I could only see her back as she studied it.

"This one's my favorite," she said, still hugging herself.

I couldn't hold back anymore. That felt like an invitation. Like she missed that time too.

I walked over to her and put my arms around her and leaned down to kiss her neck like I had done hundreds of times before. I prayed she wouldn't stop me.

I felt her knees buckle, responding to my touch and I felt like yelling in triumph that she was still as affected by me as I was her. She let out a tiny gasp, making me feel powerful as all hell, and then she quickly found my mouth.

She turned in my arms and we clung to each other, equal parts passionate and frantic.

I felt myself picking her up and she wrapped her legs around me.

Her hands were exploring all over me, she smoothed a hand through my hair and it felt like heaven. I held on to her for dear life.

She broke the kiss, "but your hand."

I took the opportunity to pay more attention to her neck, her weakness. She let another breathless sound escape.

"s'fine," I told her. It did feel a little strained inside the f'ing cast she was practically sitting on, but I didn't give a shit. This was so much more important.

I eased towards my bed and laid her down.

"This okay?" I was practically holding my breath.

She nodded urgently and grabbed my neck to bring me closer again.

"God, I can't believe this is happening," I said in awe of her and the moment. I was so happy I could cry. I leaned down and kissed her again and eased my good hand up her back under her shirt and groaned. I hated myself for the damn cast getting in the way.

I pulled back then and reached for the hem of her t-shirt. She froze and touched my hand.

"Wait," she sounded breathless.

I looked at her flushed face which held a nervous look. I waited for her to explain, to tell me what to do. We'd come so far, we both wanted this, needed this.

"I… don't look the same," her cheeks flamed, and I could see reservation sliding into her eyes, but the greatest relief washed over me.

"That's what you're nervous about? I thought you changed your mind about me," I told her.

She touched my face. Rubbing her thumb under my eye, then feeling my scar. I kissed her hand.

"Baby, I swear to God you are more beautiful than ever."

"I had a baby," she said slowly.

"And he's awesome as fuck," I told her with conviction.

She was still hesitating, "I have... stretch marks."

It killed me that she thought I'd care about something so natural and beautiful. She had never been self-conscious with me before. This again, was something I blamed myself for. I should've been by her side all these years giving her confidence and reassurance.

I touched the end of her shirt again, "Can I?"

She bit her lip and gave a nod.

I lifted her shirt over her head.

"God Jules. So fucking beautiful," I said as earnestly as I could. I needed her to realize just how fucking perfect she was. How perfect we were together.

I trailed kisses from her stomach all the way up to her face.

33 JULES - PRESENT

We laid in each other's arms, crashing down together and listening to the laughter and howling from the pool in the backyard. Laying in his arms felt like home. The late afternoon sun's golden rays were spreading into the room lazily and I wished I could stay here with him forever. I didn't want the outside world to interfere with us again.

I kissed his chest and looked up at him.

He looked so serene in that moment. The boy I loved had turned into a larger-than-life man, and now he was here with me again.

"I still love you," he choked out. Tears were in the corner of his eyes. In all the years that we were together, I'd never seen him cry before. "I never stopped. I don't even care if that's not how you feel, I want you to know Julianna."

It was my turn to tear up.

"My heart has always been yours, Greyson. For a while I didn't know if I was afraid to love someone else or if I just gave you all I had," I told him. "But I think once you love someone so fully, the way I loved you, you can't just stop loving or turn it off. It doesn't just go away. I think everyone you love forever carries a little of your love with them. And I didn't hold back with you. I gave you my whole heart. There was never anything left for anyone else." I paused; I didn't want to say what I was thinking then.

He could sense I was holding back.

He brushed a piece of hair behind my ear. He was waiting me out just like he'd done as a kid.

"That's also why it was so hard for me after us. I was completely broken. I couldn't understand how you could just put a stop to it."

His eyebrows drew together, "I didn't stop Jules."

I needed to get it all out and power through or else I never would.

"I watched your first game with the Titans. I knew I lost you, but I couldn't stop loving you. I actually hated that I couldn't turn it off."

"But Why," his voice cracked and he looked pained, "why did you marry him then?"

I grimaced. It clearly hurt him. I took a deep breath. I knew he was bound to ask about Kevin. It affected him, but I hoped it was something he could understand. In the back of my mind, I knew that I would be so hurt if he married someone else. That was the one guilty relief I felt… that he stayed single.

"Honestly, I was stuck. One minute I thought I was going to Texas with you and the next thing I knew I was pregnant and alone and 22 with no money and no job."

He was still holding me, so I went on.

"Looking back, I was so depressed. My grandparents should've been watching me, but instead I was drinking way too much and calling Kevin just to keep my company, which was shitty of me, but I paid for it. I told my grandparents I had gotten pregnant and they wanted me to get rid of it. I couldn't. I was already so depressed; it would've killed me. They gave me an ultimatum- marry Kevin or be cut off. I didn't really have a choice because I wanted what was best for my baby."

He rolled away from me then and sat up on the edge of the bed, his back turned towards me. I missed his warmth immediately.

"I wasn't best? Why wouldn't you have tried to contact me?" His face was in his hands and his voice sounded strained. "I would have been there for you. I would have helped you. You didn't give me a chance." He said each sentence pointedly.

I was afraid to move toward him; to touch him, I had to explain it to him.

"What was I going to tell you? I already thought you didn't want to be with me. Then you'd magically want me back after I'd gotten pregnant with someone else's baby? I figured you were better off without me at that point. The pregnancy was the nail in the coffin of our relationship for me. I figured there was no turning back, but I knew I'd never love anyone the way I loved you."

He was quiet. He stood then and closed his eyes with his good hand.

He shook his head, "I would've helped you. But Jesus. You were depressed… that we broke up… and I didn't even break up with you!" He looked at me with a mixture of grief and anger over what had happened. "I was going to propose to you."

That felt like a punch to the gut. I had wanted that so bad. But we had to find a way to move past it. We both needed to forgive each other and ourselves for what had happened when we were so young.

"Hey…c'mere," I patted the bed next to me up by the headboard.

He didn't budge. He was not done with the topic.

"I don't know how that happened Jules. I keep reliving it. I have been for the past nine years. I tried so hard to see you after the accident and then I went back to your house and everything was gone. It was like you turned into a ghost. I called like crazy – no response. I had no clue where the in the world you were. I figured if you wanted to be with me, you'd find me. It's not like I was that hard to find." His chest was rising and falling quickly.

I smoothed the bed in front of me.

"I had to leave because everything reminded me of our relationship. My phone was wrecked in the accident, but my new one was my same number…all I got were those breakup texts that said we were bad for each other...and to 'just stop.'"

I stopped then, realizing what I'd just said. His head snapped to meet mine then. He realized it too.

"You weren't given the same phone back?" He asked. His face turned dark, looking ready to murder.

"Who the FUCK," He roared, "gave you a new phone?" He demanded as much as he questioned. I'd never seen him so angry before, and it shocked me. It seemed he was angry at me…

"I.. D-don't," I stammered, trying to search through my memory while he paced the room like an angry lion.

He slammed both hands against the door, then held his cast against his chest, "ow, fuck."

I was frozen, staring at him and how affected he was. He was such a large and powerful man, but I'd never seen him exert any type of force off the ice. Had his gentleness been replaced with violence?

I wanted, no, needed to live the rest of my life in peace.

He turned and saw the shock in my eyes and regret washed over his.

"Jules, Baby, I'm sorry…"

I shook my head at him and tried to clear my throat.

"It's okay… it just doesn't matter anymore. Who's at fault, I mean. Because we made it back to here. Just please don't…please don't..." I almost cried as I said it and I hated myself for sounding so scared.

He nodded like a little boy being shamed and he came to kneel in front of me.

"I promise, I won't. I don't want to be apart. Do you still want everything with me?" his eyes pleaded with me.

I knew deep down that I could never say no to him.

I traced his jawline like I'd done hundreds of times. He closed his eyes and turned his cheek to kiss my hand.

"Want to join our pancake breakfast tradition tomorrow?"

34 JULES - PRESENT

I looked over at a sleeping Grey. He was such a handsome guy. His strong, razor-sharp jawline covered in scruff contrasted with how at peace he looked in his sleep.

I smoothed a finger over his eyebrow with the hole in it. He had such a tough exterior, but he was filled with compassion and love. I'd learned so much by the fact that he was here. Yes, we had broken up and it wasn't either of our faults. But he didn't have a child with someone else… I had. That did change things. My child would come before him. He had to know that.

But this. This kind of morning was a dream come true to me. Canyon sleeping comfortably in his room down the hall. And this man, with his arm draped over my stomach making me feel cherished and deserving. It brought tears to my eyes. It seemed he always wanted to be touching me these last few days, and that was alright with me. We had time to make up for. And I wanted to belong with him.

He had to leave my bed soon though. I didn't want Canyon knowing he was sleeping over...

I wasn't sure what Canyon thought was going on. I myself didn't really know. We hadn't talked about titles… it didn't seem right to just call him my boyfriend at this point. He meant so much more to me. In my head I'd always called him the one, my soul mate. But I couldn't come to say that to him in fear that it would scare him away. I wasn't sure where his head was exactly. I knew he wanted to be with me… but would he want to be a family? I didn't want to introduce him into Canyon's life as something more than a coach or friend just to have that change potentially down the line. Canyon had already had so much interruption and adjustment in his little life so far, and I still wasn't sure if I would be able to handle another adjustment of that kind either…

But Canyon had to notice that Grey had been spending a lot of time with us these past few days. He just didn't know that Grey was staying the night.

The first night Grey had stayed over I whispered to him that he needed to leave and the bonehead just didn't understand.

I pulled him away from the COD video game he'd been playing with Canyon and Smitty on the couch. Ashlie was mad at Smitty for some reason and he was apparently hiding out here. I could hear Max, and little Troy in the background, who they were playing against.

Grey had his video game headset on when I pulled him into the kitchen.

He looked down at me expectantly, "Babe, you're gonna make me lose."

I smirked at my large man-child. Some things didn't change.

"I can't talk seriously to you with that on," I joked. "But you can't stay tonight and it's getting late," I told him, cutting my eyes over to the living room where Canyon and Smitty were side-by-side engrossed in the game and chatting through the headset to the other man-child and Troy.

His face fell and he frowned down at me, "You don't want me to?"

"No, I do," I said quickly and touched his chest.

He gave an easy boy-ish smile and a wink, "Then I'm totally staying."

I swatted at him, "I mean I don't want Canyon seeing you sleeping over here, okay? It's not really appropriate."

His eyebrows drew together and he sucked on his top lip, thinking.

I popped a hip out and raised my eyebrows, waiting for him to challenge me. I was standing my ground on this. For one, I didn't want Canyon getting hopeful about this, and two, I felt like it was inappropriate for him to see a guy that didn't have a title sleeping over. If Canyon saw him staying, I wouldn't know how to explain it to him, so it was obviously easiest to just avoid the situation for now.

He cocked an eyebrow at me, "lookin real sassy there, little mama."

I shook my head at him, "laying down the law, bud."

"My girl, calling me bud!" He whisper-yelled in amusement. "That's it." He eyes flashed and he tore his headset off. Before I knew it, he wrapped his good arm around my waist and hoisted me over his shoulder.

"Oh my God!" I yelled.

"Shhh!" he urged.

We both looked over to Canyon and Smitty again. Canyon was staring at the tv. Smitty wagged his eyebrows at us.

I spanked Grey, but he didn't care.

"Ooh, feisty. You want a spanking too?" Grey whispered.

I gave up fighting. There's no way I could win against his vice-like grip.

Next thing I knew Grey had taken me in the guest bedroom. He locked the door, turned quick and then dumped me onto the bed.

"Babe," he grumbled in a husky voice. "When you get all mom bossy on me… I need you."

I couldn't help but laugh at his antics. I wanted him too.

He climbed over me quickly, making the antique bed creak under his weight.

"Shh," I warned. It felt like we were stealing time like we did as teenagers.

We laid there cuddling until we heard Smitty and Canyon's voices floating in from the kitchen.

"Your mom keep any good snacks here, kid?" Smitty asked.

"Ehhh… she's on a diet… so only gross healthy stuff," Canyon said.

"Jesus, does she even let you eat real cereal? I'm gonna have to buy you some real shit."

I rolled my eyes and found Grey frowning at me. He lifted the sheets up and looked down at my body. I immediately grabbed them back and gave him a look.

He shook his head at me and whispered against my shoulder, "You're beautiful." His words tingled against my skin.

When he said it, I felt it. He made me feel cherished, he always had. It was such a change from Kevin who treated me with so much disinterest it stripped me of confidence for years after I'd had Canyon.

I stretched to kiss his jaw. This amazing man who made me feel so loved. We hadn't said it since that first time, but he made me feel it so strongly.

"What you see is because I eat healthy, dummy," I told him.

"As long as I'm your dummy," he said against my lips and reached around my waist with his one hand, pulling me on top of him.

"Okay, so what's the plan here?" I asked, looking down at his face.

He sucked on his top lip again, his thinking face. I smoothed a hand over his scruff. He had one splotch of blond-ish hair, which I was happy hadn't changed. He was annoyed by it in college, but I always thought it gave his face more character.

"How about I pull a Romeo and just climb into this window here and then come up to your bedroom after?" He leaned back to look into my eyes as he proposed.

"Ehh…" I thought it over, "I really don't want to leave anything unlocked or open… it's just me and Canyon here."

"Babe," he rolled his eyes at me, imitating me for sure. "You don't have to worry about that. I'll be here to protect you guys," he pulled his good arm up and flexed it.

It was my turn to roll my eyes again. Although, he really had filled out nicely. While he was always strong in college, he was now manly strong. He was much thicker, like he really could take on anyone.

"How about you just give me a key then?" He asked hesitantly with raised eyebrows. "Too forward?"

I inwardly grimaced and hoped I didn't show anything on the outside. I didn't want to make him feel bad, but I couldn't handle the possibility of him ever giving a key back to me… and I was still afraid of that. I still wasn't sure if he knew what being with me now would mean. It wouldn't just be me. He'd have to be a step-father as well. I wasn't sure if he wanted to take on a family man role right away. He had always said he wanted to though… but he could have any girl out there in the world with zero strings attached… why would he settle for a mother in her thirties who would always have interference from her son's father. Even if Kevin left us alone about our relationship, what if he did step into our family and decide it was too much for him? I was trying to enjoy this while it lasted. Our relationship reached the final buzzer before, and I felt lucky to have this little bit of overtime with him… but I wasn't looking forward to the next buzzer.

He could tell I was hesitating, but I wasn't sure what to say.

He smoothed a large hand over my hair and kissed my forehead.

I laid my head against his chest, listening to his steady, strong heartbeat.

"Baby, I am here to stay," he said firmly, as though he could read my mind. "Unless you kick me out, I want to be with you, okay?"

I nodded against his chest. His words made me want to cry. I wanted to trust him completely, but I was still holding back.

Grey had a key to our house ever since that night though. He knew Canyon's bedtime was 9pm, but the kid usually weaseled another half hour out of me, so Grey usually showed up around 10:30.

One night Canyon and I had fallen asleep while watching a movie in the living room.

I woke up completely panicked when Canyon wasn't next to me, but after a quick scan, I found Grey carrying Canyon up to his room with an apologetic look on his face. My heart swelled at the sight. Canyon was too heavy for me now, and I missed those days of carrying him to his bed. I was happy I could witness my baby looking like a baby again. He was so wise for his little eight-year-old self that sometimes I forgot he was only a second grader. And to see Grey step into a dad-like role completely melted my heart. He was already acting like more of a father than Kevin ever did. But seeing it made me hope for things I had no business hoping for… like for Canyon to have siblings… and for Grey to be a father. I needed to ease those things out of mind. That was a dream I'd had for a long time, but I couldn't allow myself to hope for it. If it didn't work out, I couldn't hide myself away from the world like I did as a 22-year-old girl.

In the back of my mind, I knew that I was afraid of feeling completely vulnerable with Grey again. I knew it wasn't his fault, but for some reason I was still guarded.

…But this morning, I knew I'd let Grey stay too long, because I heard noise from out in the hallway, alerting me that Canyon had woken up earlier than usual.

As much as I hated to, I urgently tried to wake Grey up.

He was always the heaviest sleeper. One time in college I tried to wake him up to ask where his toilet paper was because it was missing from his bathroom, and I got babble for like five full minutes and almost peed myself.

I tried to shake his body, but he was heavy.

I patted his face a couple of times, but still nothing.

I could hear Canyon's feet padding the floor coming towards us.

"Shit, shit, shit," I winced as a shirtless and pajama pants clad Canyon flew open the door and ran towards my bed.

He quickly jumped up on it and stood looking down over Grey and I with a confused look on his little face.

Grey appeared still sleeping even though Canyon was bouncing the mattress under him. I looked from him to Canyon.

Grey's eyes flew open and in an instant, he mock wrestled Canyon into a headlock and was ruffling his hair.

I gaped at him. What a scoundrel. He totally faked being asleep so he could stay here.

But Canyon was laughing, so I guess things were kind of okay.

God. I internally slapped myself in the face. I should've forced him out the door way earlier to avoid this.

"Alright, alright," I told the boys to calm them a bit. "Watch your hand, Grey," I warned. He had complete disregard for the fact that he had a cast on.

"Okay, Mom," Grey's voice was laced with annoyance, but he flashed me a genuine smile.

Canyon had him pinned down then.

"Ya got me, little man," he grunted.

Canyon looked down at him, I could tell his little wheels were turning behind those playful eyes.

"Why are you here, Coach?" He asked curiously.

Grey cut his eyes over to me.

"Can I let you in on a secret?" He asked Canyon while still keeping eye contact with me. I gave me a warning look and shook my head.

Canyon nodded at him.

"I love your mom. I am completely and absolutely in love with Julianna Louise Hurley and I have been since I was 16," he told him matter of factly.

I felt like the breath was punched out of me. I couldn't believe he just told him that.

An awkward silence seemed to last for a full minute. Canyon just stared between Grey and I, and I held my breath, waiting for the worst.

But then laughter erupted from Canyon. Deep, full belly laughter, and he shrieked, "What?!"

I shrugged my shoulders at Grey and pulled a face. I guess that wasn't so bad.

"Your mom's a hottie, kid," Grey said, throwing me a wink.

"Ohh too far, coach! That's my mom!" Canyon yelled, fake gagging then.

I grabbed up my robe from the floor in my bathroom. I heard Canyon and Grey whispering to each other, and it made me smile that they got along so well.

"I'll make some coffee and breakfast for you boys," I told them.

"No, we got it!" Canyon called, and then the two of them were racing off down the hallway.

35 GREY - PRESENT

Happiness. That's what I was feeling. It was foreign to me for so long, but I was feeling joy now. I felt more alive than I had in years. These past few weeks were such a stark contrast to how I'd lived the past nine years, just bitterly going through the motions.

But now I had people to care about and people who cared about me. It was an amazing feeling.

I was basically living at Jule's house at this point. The past two weeks I'd spent every night with the two of them, and I knew I could live like this forever.

I was making moves during the day, becoming an assistant coach for League's development program. They basically had kids all day-running an online education program so that they could be at the rink and on the ice as much as possible through the day. This was of course only in addition to coaching Canyon's team.

Jules was making moves too. Max convinced her to pick up a couple shifts of coaching Learn to Skate with the toddlers during the day.

It was surreal to see her on the ice at the League. It was like we made it back to where we should've been in the first place. Here and together.

Max was rolling onto the ice driving the Zamboni. He pulled his beanie on over his shaggy hair and was beaming at me with his missing tooth smile. What a bum. I shook my head at him and ushered a couple of the tweens off the ice.

I skated over to Max and gave him a fist bump awkwardly across my body with my left hand. I couldn't wait to go back in and get this damn cast off.

"What up, man?" I asked him.

"This is my favorite part of the job," he laughed.

"Jesus. You're a hillbilly."

"You know it, son," he said, beeping the high pitch horn of the zam. He looked down at me with a more serious expression then. "So how're things goin with Jules?"

I couldn't help but smile when he said her name.

"I really can't believe it man," I told him.

"So… like wedding bells and you being called Daddy in the future?" he smirked.

"I've thought about it… but I'm not sure if she wants all that again, ya know?" I told him honestly. I really didn't know. I liked how things were. I could tell she drew a line in the sand where we were and I didn't want to push her… but I did want my ring on her finger. I still did see kids together in our future… and having a house together. My house was starting to feel like a waste of a purchase because I was spending all my time by her. It would be weird to have both of them sleepover my place.

Max looked perplexed, "Don't all women want that?"

"Hell if I know," I told him.

"I'll ask Paige to ask her," he winked at me.

I started to argue but he zoomed away from me, probably not safe for him to be in charge of that specific aspect of the rink.

I shook our conversation out of my head. Jules was on the other sheet of ice. I wanted to catch a little bit of her.

She was so graceful even when she was just moving to help a kid stand up. It made me feel like a chick thinking about it, but the way she was helping the little two-years-olds made me want to have one of our own together.

I shoved the possibility of having a family away for so long because I couldn't see it with anyone but Jules. Now that we were together, I didn't want to just pick up where we were as kids, I wanted more… I just hoped she felt the same way.

I walked through the skate-safe rubber hallway between the two rinks quickly and hopped onto the figure skaters' ice. I laughed to myself thinking of how much trouble I would've been in if I'd done this as a kid. I guess there were some perks to being old.

Jules was so into her lesson with a couple baby hockey players that she didn't even see me.

I skated up behind her, wrapped an arm around her waist, causing her to let out a surprised shriek, and twirled her around.

"What a hot coach," I whispered, and felt her body relax against mine.

I set her down. Even on skates she was so tiny. She sighed and I patted her head.

"Sorry babe, you're just so pick-up-able, I had to. Stay in that coaching outfit later," I said and wagged my eyebrows at her. She was shaking her head at me and fighting back laughter. I skated around her and went to pay attention to her kids then. Just to get 'em a little riled up for her.

36 JULES - PRESENT

After a shut-out morning game at the League, Grey had invited the entire team over his house for a barbeque and fun in the pool.

Smitty was manning the grill while Max and Grey and a couple other dads were playing pool basketball against the boys.

I couldn't keep my eyes off him. He was so incredibly tall, ripped, and tan. Maybe dad-bods were in… but looking at the other dads compared to him… no one could even come close. He still had the full athlete bod. My heart fluttered when watching how care- free and happy he was- he became a kid again when playing with the boys. And I loved the way he treated and included Canyon. It was like Canyon was one of the guys versus just a kid, and I could tell Canyon loved it. No one was criticizing him, instead, Grey made sure Canyon was always on his team, making Canyon feel like he was on top of the world. Grey had a way of making you feel that way, I knew it well. But damn. He was practically glistening in the late afternoon sun.

I internally slapped myself for ogling him in front of the whole party. I turned away from the pool and continued trying to keep up with all the trash the munchkins were leaving around. I didn't want Grey to have to deal with a huge clean up after.

I grabbed a garbage bag and was moving around his huge patio.

I felt him before he spoke. His rough, wet cast brushed down my arm.

"You should be enjoying yourself with the other moms," he said in a concerned tone. "Are you having fun?"

He was leaning over me dripping water on me.

"Yes, you throw quite the barbeque Greyson Scott," I turned to him with a smile and pushed him back a bit, "and I don't mind. But is that cast supposed to get wet?"

He had water droplets streaming down his body and water clung to his long eyelashes making them look even more full. His St. Christopher medallion on his gold chain shone bright in the sun. I didn't have to look to know what it was. He never took it off. He was devastated when he lost it in the ocean at 20, only to be the luckiest guy and grab it out of the water five minutes later.

He took the trash bag away from me and slung a wet, heavy arm over my shoulder. Giving me a boyish smile, he said, "you worry too much, Juju. I get it off tomorrow… and you know what that means."

I cocked an eyebrow at him.

He leaned in to whisper, "I get to make love to you with two hands… just imagine how much louder you'll be screaming my name, baby."

I felt a shock course through my body, emitting from low. My face was heating up fiercely, and my cheeks were without a doubt turning bright red and he totally noticed.

I could smell the beer on his breath. He was definitely feeling the alcohol a bit to be so outspoken.

He dipped close to me, "I love it when I get you all hot and bothered," he said in a low grumble. "I love that I still have that effect on you," he added in a more serious tone. He moved away from me then and moved towards the cooler. I immediately missed his presence in my personal space.

He grabbed two Coronas out of the cooler and handed one to me, just like he had so many times in the past.

I shook my head and looked up at him, "I have Canyon." I really didn't drink much anymore, besides the occasional glass of wine at dinner or the end of the day. My mom radar was always on, and I didn't mind at all, in fact, I preferred it that way. That's why Kevin didn't even try to get more than partial custody of Canyon, he was still in frat boy mode half the time. I sometimes did think it would be nice to have a night out though.

"I have chatted with Mrs. Troy's mom, whatever the hell her name is," he countered playfully. In the back of my mind, I liked how he didn't pay attention to her tall blonde figure the way Kevin had. Even if I didn't want to admit it to myself, I wanted all of his attention. "I already asked if she could take Canyon home and baby-sit tonight. They loved the idea of a sleepover, they were like jumping out of their skin," he smirked.

That was definitely more of a dad move- making sure Canyon would be alright instead of just expecting me to be free for him. It was a little different having someone else make plans... but I appreciated it.

His eyebrows drew together, "I hope that's alright," he added quickly.

"Oh, yeah," I assured him. "But what's happening tonight?" I hesitantly accepted the beer he was still holding towards me.

He shook his head at me and flashed his heartbreaker smile with all his confidence back in place, "A surprise."

37 GREY - PRESENT

I think she thought that I'd forgotten. Silly girl, I never forgot.

Every year that we weren't together, I went out with random guys from whatever team I was on and drank this night away until I blacked out. Because this date, her birthday, inevitably made me think about her and it was too painful. It was the fact that I knew she was somewhere in the world celebrating and I didn't get to be a part of it. It cracked my heart open. I shoved all memories of her in a little box in the back of my mind, but that box bust open every September 29th.

But this year would be different. Jules turned 32 at midnight and I wanted it to be memorable for her. I wanted it to be her best birthday.

I recruited Paige, Max, Smitty, Ashlie, and Canyon to all help celebrate. Canyon's part didn't come in until tomorrow though- we were making pancakes for her- the special kind with the tiny marshmallows.

I'd taken Canyon to the store with me earlier in the week to pick out a necklace. It was simple and elegant and so very much Jules with just a single white diamond hanging from a silver chain.

Canyon was thoroughly pleased with the purchase. The only thing that bugged me was the fact that he said he usually just made his mom a homemade card because his dad never took him shopping for her and never gave her a cake. The fact that she hadn't been dotted on and cared for pissed me off so damn much that I felt the urge to punch another wall harboring inside of me. What a son of a bitch to have a baby with a woman and then keep her as a wife just to treat her like shit. I wished like hell I could turn the clock back, but I needed to let go of the anger and move forward and make sure she was treated the way she deserved.

My plan for tonight was to go out on the town with her, treat her to a five-star dinner and then go dancing and get absolutely shit-faced and have the most fun. We'd finish the night up with some Taco Bell like we had in our early 20s… but this time we wouldn't be crashing in a crappy dorm room, but at my home.

Right after the barbeque, Paige and Ashlie helped me pick out my outfit because I was kinda nervous. They picked dark wash jeans and a nice button-down. It was a bit busy for my taste, but apparently it was the "in" style. Jules usually just saw me in sweats. As much as we'd been hanging out the past couple of weeks, we hadn't gone on an official date; it had been more of hanging around with her and Canyon, which I loved, but I was excited to get some time with just her tonight when she was off mom-duty.

I rang Jules' doorbell and watched through the glass paneling as she came down the stairs and it just about knocked the breath out of me.

She opened the door shyly and peaked around it, "It's weird not having Canyon race me for the door," she said quietly.

I stepped inside and looked her up and down. She looked drop dead gorgeous tonight. I didn't give her much to go on in terms of dress, or time to get ready- only about an hour between the end of the barbeque and when I picked her up, but it didn't really matter. She could be in her pajamas and I'd still find her the most attractive woman in any bar. But tonight, she had on an off the shoulder little dark red dress that hugged all her curves. She pinned her long, wavy hair to one side, so it ran down her one shoulder and was so long it reached her boob. It was light brown at the top and went to an almost blonde at the bottom. The left side of her neck and shoulder were exposed, and damn if I didn't find everything down to her toes sexy.

"What? This okay?" She asked nervously.

I gave a solemn nod, "Perfect. I'm going to have blue balls all night," I told her, causing her to cackle. She was never one to hold back her true laughter and it made me chuckle.

"My girl, c'mere," I pulled her into me and looked down at her, rubbing her bare arms. "Happy birthday."

Surprise registered on her face and she cocked her head to the side, "Well, not until tomorrow."

"You mean midnight," I corrected her. "Going to give you the best birthday," I told her matter of factly.

"Is that so, Mr. Scott?" Her eyebrows lifted. I loved holding her tiny body against mine. "Remember my 21st? That was your doing," She bit her lip and shook her head.

I looked up at the high foyer ceiling and thought back… her 21st...

I snapped my neck down, "Oh, shit, that was 21?" I asked her with the sudden flash of a memory of me throwing her over my shoulder and hauling her out of a Windsor bar and holding her hair back that night in the shitty motel room. We went to Canada so we could all drink. That was our first official bar night together because she'd been too nervous to go out before then. She was way more of a light weight than we'd both expected at the time.

I cracked a smile at the memory, and she continued to shake her head.

"I forgot about that one," I told her. "Well, if you need me to hold your hair back tonight, I am at your service," I said valiantly.

She rolled her eyes, "I learned how to hold my liquor in this past decade."

"We'll see about that, Mom," I gave the end of her hair a tug, and must've brushed her boob in doing so, causing her to freeze up and release a quick breath. I felt the heat rising in me, but I'd have to ignore it for now, "No bra tonight, eh? Trying to kill me, girl." I winked at her and gestured for her to exit.

38 JULES- PRESENT

I felt like all had been righted in the world. I still couldn't believe I was sitting in a booth at a bar with Paige and Ashlie while the guys were getting our drinks. Not our first drinks of the night. This was probably our fourth bar of the night.

"So, girl," Ashlie started; her excited green eyes shone brightly even in the darkened bar, "How are things between ya'll? I'm so excited about this!" Her southern accent came out more when she was drinking.

Paige looked at me in question as well.

I couldn't keep the smile off my face, "I think I'm still in shock over being with him again. I thought all this was gone for good, ya know?"

They both nodded in understanding.

"So… what are you guys? Boyfriend and girlfriend? Because things don't start over, they pick right back up," Paige pointed out. "Would you consider marriage?" She asked with a hopeful look.

I pondered that question. With my inhibitions lowered, I answered truthfully, "I always did want that with Greyson. But I'm kind of scared of wanting that. I'm fine with what we have right now."

"Hun," Ashlie looked at me straight, "I really don't think he wants to stay the way you guys are. He can't keep his eyes off you. I think he's scared you'll disappear on him again or something," she joked. "You aren't going to disappear again are you?" Ashlie gave me a warning look.

I chuckled wryly, "I'm so happy I have you guys again. I don't want anything to ruin it," I said earnestly, looking between the two of them. "It's been just me and Canyon for so long."

"Well, you're stuck with us forever now," she said, "because Canyon's calling me Aunt Ashlie and I fricken love it so much it makes me want to cry!"

"Well, even if you guys don't work it out romantically, I have a feeling we'll all be together for the rest of time," Paige winked at me.

Max squeezed his way into the booth next to me then, shoving me further in with his hip. He put an arm around me and faced Ashlie, "What doesn't make you wanna cry, Ash?" He joked.

"I am sorry for him," Paige recanted.

"Love you too, baby!" Max called over the loud bar music. He was pretty sloshed. "So, while G is up at the bar paying for all us because he's a rich ass and owes me, I would like to take credit for something."

"Oh no," Paige groaned and rubbed her temples.

"No! It's a good thing! I did a smart thing, baby! You'll be proud!"

I looked at Max curiously.

"So, I feel safe enough to let this out now, and like I said, I want the credit. So, I saw Canyon's parent permission slip for the try-out and saw Juju's name on it! So… that's when I moved Grey as the coach from the '03 team to the '07 team… and voila! Magic! I knew something fucked up happened before," he looked me in the eye. "I love both of you and you two deserve to be happy and together. We really missed you, Juju," he told me gruffly.

This big teddy bear. Max always was a hopeless romantic. I usually wasn't a touchy- feely person, except when it came to Grey that is, but I threw my arms around him and gave him a hug. He smelled like chew and beer; Paige would probably rip him a new one about the chew later tonight. I felt an overwhelming gratefulness towards him. How I ever thought he'd be holding a grudge against me I didn't know. He was one of the nicest guys I'd ever met. He'd been the one to throw us together again and I was grateful. He brought me back into the group. The feeling of being wanted was something I yearned for so long and I felt it here with these friends.

"Thank you," I whispered to him.

"No problem little Mama," Max replied in my ear.

"Why are your arms around my girl?" Greyson asked in a gruff voice.

"She's hugging me!" Max called. "We all love each other, okay?!"

"Jesus," Smitty said as he walked up behind Grey and slapped a hand on his back. "Max is just as sappy as drunk chicks. He's white girl wasted." He shook his head and placed a flight of shots on the table.

Grey ushered Max out of the booth to make some room for him. He had wanted to be next to me and touching me all night. It made me feel secure and wanted with his hand on my hip or lower back, or just in mine. I had a feeling it was just as much for him as it was for me.

He placed a beer in front of me and slid in, not realizing I'd be on his right side. I let a slight giggle out when he realized this. He was purposely having me in his left side to hold my hand and touch me without his bulky cast interfering.

"Damnit," he groaned and took a swig of his beer. He tipped his head back slightly and his Adam's apple bobbled up and down. Funny how I found the most ordinary things he did so sexy.

I took hold of his casted hand and placed it in my lap and leaned to kiss him on the cheek.

"It doesn't bother me," I told him, quietly so the others wouldn't hear. They were engrossed in a serious debate and ignoring us anyway though.

"Makes me feel like a pussy that I overreacted and did this in the first place," he said softly. His serious eyes were lined with red from the alcohol.

I smoothed out his free thumb and finger in my lap, "it made me realize though…" I looked into his dark chocolate brown eyes. "It was real. How we loved each other. Right?" I felt my voice get high with the need of assurance.

"Yes," he choked out. "It was real."

"Woah! You guys look way too serious," Max interrupted from across the booth. "Let's down these shots and hit the dance floor!"

Grey coughed out a laugh and passed the shots out.

"Toast!" Smitty yelled and drummed the table.

Grey cleared his throat, "To Jules, to her birthday, and to every other birthday of everyone's here being together as well."

I was shocked at his words. The open proclamation that he

wanted me to stay, that I was part of the group again. His words held no hesitation. He said them in a solid and almost commanding voice. I felt red creeping into my cheeks.

The rest of the group cheered.

We made eye contact then. He downed the shot without taking his eyes from mine.

He gestured to the glass in my hand, questioning if I'd accept the toast.

I was scared to want it. But I did want what he just said. I wanted it to my very core.

I closed my eyes and tossed it back and was met with more cheers from the group.

"That's my girl," Grey said with the corners of his lips turning into a naughty smile. "Dance?" I nodded and gave a surprised cry as he wrapped an arm around my waist and pulled me out of the booth.

"So, best birthday?" Grey asked with an easy smile.

We were laying facing each other in his bed with the lights out. He kept the bathroom light on and cracked the door slightly open to give the room a few lines of light, I knew this was for my benefit. I always did that when we were younger, and I still hated complete darkness. It was crazy how many of the little things he remembered.

After I'd first married Kevin, he would stagger up from bed and slam the bathroom door shut to tell me he was annoyed with it and then I'd have to lay there next to him in utter darkness. He kept distance from me in bed. We both knew the drill. We were married, but pretty much in name only. I knew he was still having sex. Just not with me. In all the years of our marriage we never once cuddled and we really didn't have sex after Canyon was born. I think it was a choice both of us made without ever speaking about it. But we'd lay in bed next to each other and I'd stare at the ceiling and wonder if this was all life would be for me.

Looking at this man across from me, I couldn't help but think how he was the total opposite, and I couldn't help but feel so overwhelmingly lucky.

I thought about my favorite birthday for a second before speaking.

"This was tied for my favorite I think," I shared sleepily.

He pouted his bottom lip out slightly, "Damn...But I just gave you like three orgasms!" He paused and cut his eyes toward me, "Did the asshole do a better job?" He didn't have to say Kevin's name for me to know who he was talking about. Since being with Grey he never once fully said Kevin Tate. I knew he hated Canyon's last name and I knew it was something that we would have to talk about because it wasn't about to change, but not tonight.

"You must be joking," I returned and patted his face. "I've never had better, and you know it."

That satisfied him and he smiled triumphantly, proud in his manhood.

"No," I closed my eyes and turned my body to allow him to be the big spoon. I nuzzled into him, relishing in his warmth. He placed a large, outstretched hand on my stomach. It was funny, our size difference made it so his hand took up my entire stomach, one of his fingers grazed the bottom of my boob and his pinky rested under the band of my undies. "The first time you said you loved me. On the floor in the rink. 17. I held onto that one."

It was true. That particular memory had become a secret that I held close to my heart. A memory I never uttered aloud, in fear that it would become tarnished or cast away as silly teen love when I know it hadn't been. It was a moment I thought of every time Kevin had made me feel unlovable.

He was silent for a minute. I enjoyed the rhythm of his breathing. I felt so relaxed and safe that I could fall asleep in a second.

"I've never said I love you to anyone else," he told me.

That sentence held so much power to me. I clung to it. It was an admission that filled me with so much love for him and I was so grateful I'd shared that secret with him.

I could tell he was waiting for me to respond. I felt his hand tense slightly against my stomach in apprehension.

"Mmm…I've said it a lot to another guy," I told him.

I felt him start to remove his hand and I snatched it back before he could. I loved him pulling me close; I wanted it to last forever.

"Canyon," I said, patting his arm with a giggle.

He let out a breath and pinched my stomach playfully causing me to jump further into him, "Brat," he said in my ear before playfully biting it.

I felt a warming joy spread inside of me in the moment.

"Me neither," I said quietly with a smile on my face. "Only to you."

He kissed the top of my head and we both relaxed into each other to sleep.

39 GREY - PRESENT

"Yes!" I shouted, making a fist as the goal buzzer sounded. The dad in the score box cued up the Griffin's goal song.

My little guys erupted in cheers and I turned to Smitty, who was also standing on the team bench, to give him a solid high five. I was still only using my left hand even though I'd gotten the cast off a couple days ago. The doctor had recommended another week in the cast, but I couldn't take it. I kind of regretted that decision though because it felt pretty damn fragile, and I was 100% babying it. I needed to man up and start using it again. I told myself the next fist bumps would be with my right hand.

The line that just scored the fifth goal of the game to break the tie against the Griffins' rivals sped towards the box to give their teammates celebratory fist bumps. I heard a bunch of the boys yelling out their celebratory "wooo!" Much higher pitched than I was used to hearing, but I was proud of how these little guys were forming such a tight-knit team. I leaned over to be included in the fist bump line, chastising myself for flinching like a pussy.

I couldn't help but be a little extra proud that Canyon was on the scoring line. The little dude had put in two goals and now just got his second assist in the game.

He was still missing the net half the time- definitely better than all the time like he had during the first game- but we needed to continue working on that shot of his. We'd been working on it in the driveway almost every day after school. Once he got that down he'd be an unstoppable force.

When Canyon's line came back on the bench, I gave them all a pat on their helmets and got ready to watch the last shift of the game.

At the final buzzer, my team flew out of the box to stampede our little goalie, who promptly collapsed into the ice, causing a dog pile to form.

I was finding that I loved coaching these little guys. It was like being able to live it again, and there was nothing better than youth hockey. Even the NHL wasn't as much fun as playing on the Griffins with my best buds.

After the game, I knew Smitty would be handling the post-game speech, so I took a minute to run to the concession stand for a bag of ice for my hand. It had started cramping up a bit and I didn't want it to get worse.

I quickly explained what I needed to the high school kid behind the counter and he nodded in awe, probably recognizing me, before turning to get the ice.

Holding the bag to my hand, I turned to head back to the locker room and almost ran over Jules.

"Woah, there, sorry," she laughed.

I pulled her closer toward me and smiled down at her, "77 was on fire today."

"The coach looked pretty good out there too," she returned with her eyes crinkling in the corners from smiling.

She looked so damn hot with barely any makeup on, just a swipe of mascara. She only took about 15 minutes to get ready this morning. I was happy that I got to have that kind of knowledge about her again. She was definitely a MILF and looked every part of it in her leggings, tidy white tennis shoes, and white baseball cap to match.

"Is that so?" I joked, tipping her hat up and leaning down to kiss her.

God I was so happy I could kiss her again. I'd never take it for granted.

She patted me on the chest and broke the kiss, "don't you need to get in there?" She said, nodding towards the locker rooms without taking her eyes off me. She looked down at my hand with a little frown then, "Is it feeling okay?"

"More than, baby. Just a little stiff," I winked to give her assurance. "We'll be out soon."

"Wanna hit up the cider mill after?" She asked hopefully.

I shook my head at her, "you just want the donuts, don't you?"

She broke into a smile, God I loved her smile.

"Yes, I'd love to take you two," I told her, and I really would.

As I turned forward to leave her, I realized we'd been watched. My eyes came up to meet Kevin Tate's. He was standing near the locker room hallway, late to go in and untie Canyon's skates.

His face gave nothing away; it was stone cold as he regarded me.

I felt my stomach twist into an angry, nervous knot and forced myself to continue walking his way.

When I reached him, I stuck my hand out to shake his even though I would've rather shit my pants than shake the slim bag's hand. He was Canyon's father and always would be, I reminded myself. I needed to make sure this relationship was at least cordial.

But he stared down at my hand smirking and he brushed past me to walk away, not even bothering to go into the locker room to chat with his kid.

I blew out the breath I'd been holding and looked toward the rink ceiling. God was testing me. I wanted to smash his teeth in.

But I truly didn't want to be the one to further strain the relationship between Canyon and his dad. At the same time, what kind of guy refused a handshake? We'd never even been introduced to one another.

I had a feeling he knew exactly who I was just as I knew who he was though.

Pushing the locker room door in it dawned on me a little too late that if he wasn't going in to see Canyon, he would be out in the lobby with Jules… I would go after her, but then Canyon would be sitting in the locker room alone- the only one without a parent congratulating him and giving him a pat on the back. No kid deserved that, and especially not him after all the hustle he put into that game. I pulled out my phone to text Jules real quick asking if everything was alright and that she should come hang in the locker room with us. At this age the kids didn't care if a mom was in the locker room, I think kids preferred it sometimes, especially after a bad game.

God. I was so pissed at the situation. Now I was worried about Jules and Canyon.

I tried to relax my face. I knew I had murder written all over it.

Opening the door, I was hit with a massive whiff of kid sweat, music blasting, and Smitty yelling over top of it about heart and hard work. That guy really got into his post-game speeches.

I forced out a smile to the boys calling out to me and smacked some high-fives as I made my way over to sit my ass down next to Canyon who was busy trying to unlace his skates.

I could see he was struggling with a double knot, and it reminded me of his age. He acted and sounded like an adult most the time, and I knew that was because he wanted to be treated like one of the guys. Sometimes it really was easy to forget he was only a second grader. He was avoiding looking at me and everyone else.

Troy was sitting next to him busily chatting away, seemingly knowing that Canyon wasn't going to respond and okay with it; he didn't expect him to and he didn't ask what was wrong. I liked the kid more for that. Troy would be a good friend to him.

I put a hand on his back, "you played an awesome game, kid."

He stopped trying to untie his skate and turned to me, his head still lowered by his skates. I could see he was holding back emotion. He sniffed and twitched his nose a bit, "Was my dad mad?"

I wasn't expecting that question and my face probably said that.

"He was," Canyon deadpanned, answering for me. "That's why he didn't come in. I missed a bunch of shots," he said quietly.

I wish I wouldn't have kissed Jules right then. Canyon was striving for any sign of Kevin's approval, and our actions stopped that. But who knew if the asshole would have even given him any praise? The kid was clearly the best on the team. Even with missing a bunch of shots, he was still the leading scorer by far, and Kevin still wasn't happy.

I got up from the bench and squatted down in front of Canyon, Ignoring the painful crack in my knees.

I pulled his skate toward me and started untying.

"Did you have fun?" I asked him.

He blew out a breath, "yeah."

"Did you try your hardest and give it your all?"

He looked at me and chewed the inside of his cheek, "yeah."

"And you got two goals and two assists. You helped put the puck in the net 4 out of the 5 times this team scored. That's pretty damn good. Better than what I could do at your age," I told him squarely.

He paused for a minute, assessing me.

"Actually?" He asked with skeptical little eyes.

"Dead serious, kid. Wouldn't tell ya that if it wasn't true. Wanna know what else?"

He nodded.

"I've played everywhere. Wanna know where I had the most fun?"

He nodded again.

"Right here."

He seemed to accept what I'd said and I helped him finish taking off his equipment in silence.

The number of kids in the locker room started to dwindle. I was trying to hurry him up a bit because I didn't want Jules out there alone with Kevin. I knew that was stupid of me to think because she'd been alone with him for nine years…and Kevin couldn't hurt her… she was the mother of his child. He had to have some kind of heart… but I had a shit feeling about the way he looked at me and refused to shake my hand. And Jules was mine to protect.

Canyon picked up his bag, struggling under the weight of it. Usually I thought this was a good thing- character building for hockey boys and all that… but I cringed thinking of how this would slow us down.

"How bout I take it this time? Your mom is dying for cider mill donuts and I don't want her to get hangry on us."

Canyon smirked up at me and nodded.

I rubbed my knuckles across his sweaty head and grabbed the bag straps from her shoulder and hoisted it up onto mine.

Smitty gave both of us knuckle punches on the way out.

"Take care of my lead scorer!" He called as we walked out.

"You mean my lead scorer?!" I rebutted.

"Jeez, guy thinks he can take over as head coach just because he gives good speeches?" I asked Canyon.

The kid laughed, amusement dancing in his eyes, so much like his mother's. Probably hearing the title of lead scorer made him feel a little more validated even if his asshole father couldn't see that.

We walked the locker room hallway chatting about the game. It wasn't until we hit the lobby and I couldn't immediately see Jules that I started to really worry.

I scammed over the tables, concession stand, vending machines, and video games… she was nowhere to be found.

Where the hell did she go? Maybe the bathroom?

I checked my phone. She hadn't texted back.

"You see her?" I asked Canyon, trying to keep my voice calm, despite the feeling of panicked rage building from my core.

"Maybe she's in Benny's or the pro shop?" He shrugged.

At least the kid was thinking. I tried to calm my mind and remind myself of all the reasons I could not punch that asswhipe's face in.

We made our way through the lobby to the entrance of Benny's and the pro-shop.

"You wanna check Benny's? Ask Paige if she's seen her?" I asked Canyon.

He gave a tough nod and ran ahead of me.

I quickly scanned the pro-shop with no success and Canyon came out of Benny's shaking his head.

"Maybe she's picking up the car?" He asked quietly with eyes darting back and forth. I could tell Canyon was getting nervous and that was my fault. I didn't want him to realize I was nervous about his father being an ass to his mother. The shitty thing about it was that he probably had already seen that happen.

"I'm sure she is, I don't know why I was freaking," I said, forcing out a chuckle.

He chuckled nervously too then and looked up at me, "yeah."

But the worry I was feeling was reflected in his eyes as well.

I started out of the rink, pretty much speed walking. Canyon had to run beside me to keep up with my long strides, but he didn't complain.

I felt like grabbing him up along with his bag I was already carrying so I could break into a run.

I couldn't see them yet, but I was already hearing them arguing from across the parking lot where Jules' car was.

As soon as they came into view, I wasn't sure if I'd made the right decision in finding them. Because I wasn't sure I could contain my anger.

Kevin had Jule's arm in a vise-like grip.

"Why the FUCK is he with my son?" He yelled, the veins in his neck were bulging and his face was a dark red as he gestured toward us with a wild arm.

"He's done with this team," he spit. "Be on the lookout for custody papers," he said with a nasty snarl, looking down at a dumbstruck Jules.

40 JULES - PRESENT

I figured he wouldn't recognize Grey... maybe he'd seen his name somewhere and had put two and two together. But still… he left me, not the other way around. I played wife for him. He decided he wanted Tammy full time and not both of us as side pieces. And I thanked God for that…He had to split half of everything with me. It was the only good outcome of us really since my grandparents pretty much gifted him all of my inheritance through the business. It hadn't been a surprise that he didn't even battle me for custody of Canyon, but he made sure I knew he could whenever he wanted… But I did not expect this level of anger from him over Grey.

Everything had been going so well… too well. I knew I shouldn't have gotten so comfortable loving Grey. It was too good to be true. If it was between staying with Grey or having Canyon, I'd choose Canyon in a second… and it looked like I was going to have to make that decision.

Kevin had a crazy possessive look in his eye, and I didn't want Canyon to see it. I wished like hell that the two of them would just walk away and give us a minute.

I gave a split-second pleading look to Grey to try to communicate this, but he was staring at Kevin with murder in his eyes.

This needed to stop before it escalated out of control.

I angled to stand in front of Grey and Canyon and moved towards Kevin, reaching out to him in a placating way.

"Can we just talk about-"

Before I could finish, Kevin forcefully shoved my arms away, so hard that I stumbled to keep from falling on the cement.

"Mom!" I heard Canyon call out. I hated that he'd just seen his dad act so aggressively toward a woman… but I was only fooling myself if I thought it was the first time.

"Touch her again and you'll be sorry," Grey said in a low voice. His voice itself was threatening. I'd never heard that tone out of him before.

I heard Kevin respond with a snide laugh, "and why would I be sorry?"

This needed to dissipate before Grey and Kevin got into it. In that case there would be no going back.

"Kevin, can we just talk about this later?" I pleaded.

"Oh bullshit, cut the innocent act, Julianna," he snapped, moving closer to tower over me. "You need to stop! This is over!" He yelled down.

That was a mistake.

Grey knew those words. I shifted my eyes over to him nervously, and it was like something clicked inside of him.

In an instant Kevin was ripped away from me. Grey pulled back and slammed his fist into Kevin's eye.

His right fist.

Grey cursed and threw Kevin onto the pavement.

But Something wasn't right. Grey was holding his right fist. And Kevin was laughing up at him.

I felt my stomach sinking.

I would in no way be able to be with Grey now. Kevin would use this against me to get custody of Canyon. And Kevin knew that.

Grey looked at me confusedly with worried eyes and I just shook my head. I couldn't muster up words for fear my face would break.

I had just gotten used to loving and feeling loved. I knew I shouldn't have gotten comfortable.

Grey tried to put an arm around me, but I held my hand up and avoided eye contact.

I couldn't bear it. I'd break down. I couldn't have him and I didn't want to pretend things would be okay. It really was over.

"Canyon we have to go," I said.

"But mom-"

"No. Get your bag. We have to go right now," I said as sternly as I could make out, but my throat felt like it was closing.

Kevin staggered up and started to walk away. He turned and gave me a wink.

I tasted bile in my throat as I took Canyon's bag and threw it in my trunk myself.

A hand touched my arm and I flinched away.

I turned to see Grey looking at me with pity swimming in his dark eyes and hated it.

His eyebrows drew together in concern and confusion but he couldn't seem to find words.

I looked down before he could see tears forming and tore away from him.

I was all motions and no second guessing then.

I quickly threw my car in reverse, backed out and drove, leaving him in the parking lot staring into my back window.

"Mom. He wanted to come with us," Canyon said quietly.

I swallowed hard.

"I know baby. But it's okay just me and you, right? It'll be okay."

I felt a little hand on my shoulder, and I hated that I flinched away from him too. I thought I had moved past that.

I tried to shake off any feelings and just breathe. We'd be fine. It would be okay… as long as it was the two of us everything would be okay.

41 GREY - PRESENT

Fuck.

Just fuck.

My hand was toast and Jules was gone. What the hell had just happened? I tried to process in my head all of what I'd just seen and heard.

Well, I had no way of getting back to my place. I'd driven here with Jules.

I had no choice but to walk back into the rink holding my hand pathetically.

Feeling completely dejected, I walked up to the concession stand asking for ice again when I felt a slap on the back.

"What up, brotha?" Max asked. He must've caught a glimpse of my hand over my shoulder because his next words were: "what did you do?" In a very disappointed voice.

I shrugged him off me, I didn't like how he was implying it was my fault.

"Had to," I grumbled.

"Oh of course," he said sarcastically. "Let's get out of the lobby before parents start questioning." Max led the way to his office and I followed behind feeling like a kid being called to the principal's office. But it was Max. He'd gotten in so much more trouble than me. And that asshole deserved it. I just couldn't grasp the rest of what I had seen...or what I had just caused. I didn't want to grasp it.

Max ushered me into the office, but I didn't budge, "I think we need Paige," I told him.

He lifted his eyebrows and blew out a breath, "Yeah, we always do. But I don't want to stress her out right now, okay?"

I brushed past him, ripped my hat off and threw it on the ground with force.

Rubbing my eyes, I took a seat. How the fuck were we having more problems? Maybe I shouldn't have tried to get everything back so quick. But it was Jules. She was worth it. So fucking worth it. There was no one else for me. I knew it. And she knew it. I could feel it in her touch and the way she looked at me. It was the same addictive way she looked at me at sixteen, making me feel like the hero in her story.

Max took a seat across from me. "Can you move it?" He asked, nodding towards my hand.

I tried to open it without cringing, but it was useless. I felt it throbbing painfully, like I'd just rebroken it.

"Well. We're going to the hospital again," Max said in a warning tone. "And I'm not taking no for an answer."

I stared at the ground, ignoring him and still processing.

"You know anything about Canyon's dad?" I asked Max.

"I mean… I think he's a mean son of a bitch from what I've seen of him around the rink… but nothing out of the ordinary for that kind. Why?"

I couldn't bear to look up at Max and admit what I was thinking, but I had to say it aloud to test the idea.

"I think…I think he hit her," I heard myself say it so quietly. It pained me to hear it. My beautiful, happy Jules who'd always cared so deeply about me. Her long beautiful hair, her smooth, pale skin, her beautifully delicate and grace filled body. I couldn't bear to think of her hurting and pretending like everything was fine. But it was making sense now. And the more I thought about it, the more the pieces were coming together. The way she'd jumped away from me when I was close to her, almost like I'd scared her just by being near. The way she flinched away when I had tried to touch her when we first started talking again. I noticed the reaction had eased away the last couple of weeks with me, but it was still something that happened with strangers. I had written it off as her just being nervous in a new setting. It had never crossed my mind that she was nervous because someone had…

"Oh my God," I said in a pained voice and dropped my head down in my hands.

We sat there like that in silence for a couple of minutes. It was agonizing to think of. While I'd be depressed and a prick over the last few years because I thought I'd been wronged, I was still living a pretty damn good life living out my dream and playing hockey. She had been treated like that in addition to feeling rejected by me.

"I don't blame you then," Max said quietly. "About your hand." He paused, "Can you keep this from Paige… for a little at least?"

"No one can know," I told him quickly and firmly. "She didn't even tell me. She wouldn't want anyone to know."

Max held my gaze and nodded. I could trust him to keep this a secret.

"You're not going to let it happen again," Max said it as a statement instead of a question. He was her friend as well.

"Max… he's the one who caused it all. He gave her that phone. He sent her those breakup texts. I'm sure of it."

42 GREY - PRESENT

I hadn't heard anything from Jules for the rest of the day. It was an abrupt change that stung. I could tell she was trying to close the door on us, but I wouldn't let her. She just didn't know that yet. I would be there for them forever. Her and Canyon.

I was fighting myself from contacting her. I knew I needed to be patient. On one hand, we'd already lost so much time together and I didn't want to lose anymore. But on the other hand, I wanted her to know I wasn't going to force her into anything. I wanted her to know she was in control. I desperately wanted her to come to me, but only on her own terms.

She didn't miss an exciting day with me anyway. I hoped they had gone to the cider mill together and enjoyed the day and some donuts. I was happy she had Canyon. I could trust that he would stick with her and know how to brighten her day and that thought at least gave me some peace as I signed out of the hospital with shitty left-handed writing.

I had rebroken my hand and was back in a cast again. At least it was shorter because my wrist was okay this time. I didn't even care. I didn't have it in me to argue with Max about not going. My thoughts were consumed by Jules and Canyon and that fucking asshole.

What had he meant when he was laughing? And what the hell was up with the way he winked at Jules?

I hadn't seen or heard of him coming around since I really started talking with Jules. Why would he come out of the woodwork now? I guessed he would always be around in some part… but he didn't seem very concerned with Canyon, so I didn't get it. And that comment about custody… I didn't understand.

I would've asked Max to have Paige ask her about everything, but Max for some reason wanted to keep Paige out of the loop. I figured we should reach out to Ashlie next so she could dig a little.

I really didn't want to be back at my house. I was terrified that Kevin would show up at Jules' place, but I didn't really have a choice. I wasn't about to force my presence on her. And my presence seemed to throw Kevin over the edge.

My house was so quiet without the two of them. They had quickly become staples in my life. I had to keep reminding myself that their absence would only be temporary.

I fixed myself some leftover pizza and grabbed a beer from the fridge to bring into my living room. I needed to distract myself from my need to text her.

I laid myself down taking up the full length of my couch and flipped on a 90s sitcom. I placed my phone on my chest, wanting it to be near just in case she did call me or need me.

At some point during the sitcom's marathon, I dozed off. I quickly searched around for my phone which had fallen off me.

Finding it between the cushions of the couch, I peered at the screen and saw Jules sent me a message.

My hands were shaking as I fumbled to open it up.

But all it read was: *Is your hand okay?*

I blew out a breath of relief. At least it wasn't about Kevin. And that showed she cared about me. Thank God.

I texted back: *Slight rebreak. Cast back on, but it doesn't matter, all good.*

Jules replied quickly: *You had to go to the hospital again? I'm so sorry.*

I chuckled to myself as I typed: *I'm becoming a frequent flyer there. Not as scared anymore*

For real?!

No. Haha. But I knew Max wasn't going to let me out of it.

Good boy, Max.

Three dots popped up but she was hesitating. I quickly typed to help her out of her own head:
I'm pretty wiped. I'm gonna get to bed babe.

All she responded with was: *Ok*

But what the hell. I knew she wasn't, I typed out my reply before overthinking: *You okay?*

Three dots popped up again and then stopped. I thought she was done for the night, but a full minute later she responded.

I miss you.

I typed with no hesitation, *Thank God. Want me to come over?*

I want you to but I'm kind of scared that he will pop over.

Then I'm coming right now, babe. I need to hold you tonight, okay?

Ok.

43 JULES - PRESENT

I was waiting in my living room for Grey in my pjs of choice: an old t-shirt of Grey's that was so big on me it acted as a nightgown.

I heard the front door start to move and I immediately tensed up. I knew it was Grey. But I was still terrified it would be Kevin, and I unwillingly held my breath.

As soon as I could tell it was Grey's body, I felt myself relax and walk into my foyer.

"Hi, babe," Grey said with a smile over his shoulder as he locked the door.

He started toward me then and went to reach for my hair, and I tensed. I could tell he sensed it and he paused.

I looked up into eyes filled with understanding.

The image of him blurred from the tears forming in my eyes.

In an instant he folded himself around me in an all-encompassing hug.

"Shh," Grey said, rubbing my back. I was trembling out of control, and I let myself fall into him and accept the only true comfort I had craved for so long. "That shits over Jules. I'm never leaving."

44 JULES - PRESENT

He said the words he was never leaving, but I knew that couldn't be true. I was stupid to text him. But I wanted this one last night with him. To feel cherished by him one more time. To be selfish. To feel open and weak and vulnerable all at the same time for one last night.

In bed, my legs parted for him naturally. He eased his way between as he came over top of me. He stared down at me with so many emotions, hunger and need and love.

"Let's go slow, baby," he said in a gravelly voice in my ear.

I watched the sunrise through my curtains next to a sleeping Grey. I didn't want him to know I was awake. I wanted to stay safely nuzzled into him. I wanted his hand that was gently placed on my stomach as he slept to stay.

But these were things I had no business wanting.

Kevin wasn't going to let this go. He texted last night before Grey arrived, telling me that if Grey and I were together, he would use Grey punching him as a way to take Canyon from me. He said Greyson Scott was dangerous and he would make sure everyone knew. Forget his new coaching position that he loved. He'd drag Greyson through the mud. Kevin would ruin both of us. And Grey didn't deserve that just for being with me. It wasn't worth it.

What really hurt was that Kevin didn't even want Canyon. He would end up sending him away to St. Jude's to be looked after. I couldn't bear it. My baby needed me as much as I needed him.

I didn't want to hurt Grey, but I knew I took from him last night.

I would say goodbye to him this morning and that would be it. Tears stung my eyes as I tried to remind myself that I didn't want this morning to be ruined and I didn't want Grey to know I was saying goodbye to him.

45 GREY - PRESENT

Jules had been very subdued when we said goodbye this morning, but I didn't want to pressure her to share what she was feeling. She was going through a lot and she didn't need me adding to it.

I had a jam-packed day. Smitty and I were helping Max organize a tournament at the League this week for the U15's. My time was split between helping Max organize shit and keeping scouts happy.

I wasn't a big fan of the schmoozing; it had never been my thing, I just liked playing hockey. But having played in the NHL, I could just stand there and nod and smile here and there and they accepted me. I ended up bragging about my team more often than not, telling them they'll have some awesome guys to watch out for in a couple of years.

I kept checking my phone all day but hadn't heard anything from Jules.

I figured the next best was Canyon. I had gifted him an iPhone a couple of weeks ago. Jules was a little if-y about giving it to him, but I assured her it didn't have internet abilities- it was only to make calls and texts. I thanked God I gave it to him because I wanted him to be able to reach out to me if Kevin ever came around. I told him so much before I had left this morning.

When Jules was getting ready, I snuck off to Canyon's room.

I wanted to tread lightly with the topic, reminding myself that I didn't know the full story. I decided to make my directions to him very vague.

I shook him slightly.

He rubbed his eyes open, "Coach?"

"Hey, bud. Make sure you call me if you or your mom ever need me, okay? I'll drop everything. Your mom might be too proud to call, so you make the call. Sound good?"

He nodded firmly, still rubbing his eyes. "It's like the crack of dawn," he complained and turned to go back to bed.

Canyon replied to my text saying that Troy was sleeping over and that's Jules was in the kitchen with Troy's mom.

That eased my worry. She was probably just busy.

Max invited all the parents and coaches to Benny's after the last game, and I figured I'd go… until Jules texted me at least. Well, I hoped she would text me again…

"Coming to Benny's?!" One of the assistant coaches of the U15 team named TJ called out to me across the lobby. TJ was only about 26 or 27 and he was still trying to make it in hockey. He was on an AHL team's roster but was out for a couple weeks with a knee injury. Max was letting him use the League to train in exchange for some coaching. TJ was a couple years younger, but he was always around the rink growing up.

"Yeah man," I slapped him five as he came nearer. "I just have to put some shit from the tournament in my car real quick and then I'll be in," I told him.

"Awesome, need any help?" He asked with eager eyes.

"You want to help take shit to my car?" I asked dubiously. No way the kid actually wanted to help with such a mundane task.

He rubbed a hand through his pretty boy hair, "I'm having lady troubles and Max said he passed the torch to you," he said sheepishly.

I laughed at that, "No, bro, I'm still having some troubles of my own. Paige is who you actually want to talk to," I pointed out.

He cut his eyes over to Benny's, "it's not weird to ask her?"

"She is the expert, man. Max is just the front man. The security guard to the love doctor, if you will," I chuckled. "But if you want to help me...?"

He grimaced and looked toward Benny's again.

"Go get help, kid," I told him. He nodded distractedly and walked off.

I exited the rink and was making my way toward my car, juggling a hockey bag of shit and trays of empty water bottles.

The other team's bus just pulled out of the parking lot, leaving it pretty empty. Most of the parents were still in the rink. The lot would be full soon, busy with parents leaving after getting their fill of chatting about the game with each other.

I set the water bottle trays down by my car to open the trunk.

What's funny is that I heard it before I felt it: The sound of a crack as I looked at the pavement.

Then pain came.

Shocking, horrible pain around my head.

My vision started to swim in and out as I staggered to stay upright.

I caught a massive whiff of what smelled like a brewery and I heard someone yelling at me from the back. I couldn't make out any words, they all sounded like they were coming from underwater.

I tried to stand back up straight and turn to face them, but couldn't because somehow, I didn't know where the ground was.

My first thought was that I wasn't supposed to have any more head injuries.

But I was on the cement then, looking under my car and black bled into my vision on all sides.

46 JULES- PRESENT

Max kept calling me, but I was determined not to answer.

That was the fifth missed call.

I needed things to end and having to explain it would just open the wound again. I needed to move on.

I would explain things to him, but I needed a couple of days to let it settle in my mind. I could not cry when breaking things off. Because I truly, deeply didn't want to break things off and Grey would just try to find solutions… and there wasn't a solution to this. I wouldn't take a gamble with custody. It wasn't an option for me.

I would surely see them at the rink, but I needed to detach.

I called Jen over for dinner and explained the situation to her and asked if she could take Canyon to practices and games for a while. It would be hard, because I loved cheering on my boy, but it needed to happen. I gave her a very skimmed over explanation. She was skeptical but accepted.

She did ask if she could go after Grey, which annoyed the hell out of me, but that's the kind of person she was, so I let it go. And it didn't hurt that I knew Grey wasn't interested in her.

But Max needed to stop calling.

I knew Grey was probably the one calling.

All of a sudden, I jumped.

Someone was banging on my door.

It was 11pm.

I sent up a quick prayer to God. Anyone but Kevin.

Canyon and Troy ran out of the bedroom. I ushered them with my hand to go back, but Canyon seemed to stand up taller and shake his head, defying me.

I was paralyzed by nerves until I heard a voice from behind the door.

"Juju! It's me, Max!"

That jerked my body into action and I opened the door for him quickly.

"Jesus. Will you two ever stop being so damn difficult?" He grumbled jokingly, but the joke didn't make it up to his serious eyes.

He peered up the stairs, seeing Canyon and Troy and then turned to me. "Grey's in the hospital," he said quietly.

I was not expecting that. I felt my stomach drop and fear crippled my body.

"Why?" I was almost too scared to hear the answer.

He looked again to the kids, wondering how he should phrase what he was going to say.

"Parents found him on the ground in the parking lot. He was hit with something in the head."

I immediately turned to grab my purse and keys.

"Which hospital?"

"He wasn't supposed to have any more concussions," Max said quietly.

"I know," I snapped at him. "Which hospital?" I demanded.

Max was still holding back.

"Why the hell would you come here and then not tell me?!" I demanded, hating the screech in my voice.

He avoided eye contact with me as he answered.

"I saw him checking his phone nervously all day."

I felt red creeping into my face and guilt slammed into me.

"You know I love you," he said gently. "And I know you've been through your own hell too. But Jules… Don't come if you aren't planning to stay with him. Don't do that to him."

47 GREY - PRESENT

I opened my eyes to a bright room with sun streaming in. My head was pounding as I looked around and took stock.

Looking down I noticed I was in a hospital dress and dread washed over me like a bucket of cold water.

"Hiya handsome," Paige said as she entered the room. I just stared at her. "You feeling okay?" She asked in a chipper voice. Her happiness was rubbing off on me the wrong way.

"Where-?" I realized with one word that it hurt my head to speak. I lowered my voice to a whisper, still wincing. "Why am I here?"

My brain was extremely foggy and I hoped I wasn't stuck like this. I struggled to think back to the last thing I remembered.

The parking lot.

I started to get up, but a pain shot through my side. I looked down the hospital dress and noticed I was taped up.

"You have broken ribs, bud," Max said, coming up behind Paige. He rubbed his jaw. His eyelids looked heavy, like he hadn't slept. He was still in the clothes he wore to the tournament, so I doubted I was out longer than the night.

But staring at Max and Paige from the hospital bed, a bad sense of déjà vu set in. Why were they here and not Jules?... Surely she knew I was here... they must've told her.

The two of them looked at each other with grimaces and avoided looking at me.

She wasn't here again.

I couldn't go through this. Not again.

I brought my hands up to my head and closed my eyes. I wished I'd been hit harder because I didn't want to remember her and not have her. I didn't want to live alone again.

"Get out," I grunted without looking at them. They didn't budge. "Get! Out!" I yelled and then cringed, closing my eyes against the pounding in my head.

"We just wanted to give you this…"

I whipped my head around at the sound of that tiny voice and immediately regretted it. It felt like my brain was loose and rattling around in my head.

Standing there was a shocked looking Canyon holding a card and a Tupperware box. Jules was behind him with her hands on his shoulders wearing a look of worry on her face.

"Don't worry, he just thought you guys didn't come," Paige said with a warning look at me.

Immediate relief coursed through my body. I took a couple deep breaths to try to steady the way my head was feeling.

"Canyon, bud," Max said. "How about you come with us to find Smitty and Aunt Ashlie while Grey let's his brain catch up a bit."

Canyon gave a nod of approval, walked toward me and gave me his presents.

I ruffled his hair, "thanks, kid. I'm sorry for yelling," I said quietly.

He seemingly held no grudge, and I thanked God for that. He put out his little fist for a knuckle punch, causing me to painfully chuckle.

I heard Max whisper to Jules, "I'm glad you came." And then they were out.

"You weren't going to come?" My face cracked with emotion.

"I was afraid," Jules told me. "Kevin wasn't going to let it slide that you hit him. He was going to try to take Canyon away from me. But… Thank God… Max had new security cameras installed in the parking lots to scare away kids from drinking out there… and they caught the whole thing. Kevin knocked you out and kicked you when you were down. I didn't watch. Max just told me… but please…" She stepped closer to me and lightly touched my arm. "Please press charges…"

I paused a long moment. "It's Canyon's father, are you sure?"

She nodded and her eyes started to look glassy with tears. She turned away from me. It pained me that she felt she needed to hide emotions from me. She never had in the past. It would be my mission to give her the safety and confidence in me that she needed to share everything once again.

"I wasn't strong enough to before," she closed her eyes and it killed me. I needed to hold her.

"C'mere, babe," I patted the bed next to me and scootched over a bit.

"No, I don't want to hurt you," she replied in a quieter decibel that tried to cover the shakiness in her voice.

I pouted my lip out. She couldn't deny me in a hospital bed.

But she was standing firm.

I leaned over the bed and planted a hand against her hip. I felt a small triumph in the fact that she didn't jump away from me, she just looked at me in confusion.

I took that as permission.

Letting out a grunt, I pulled her up and into the bed.

"Grey, your ribs!"

Once I had her tucked close to me, I took a few long breaths.

Her long delicate fingers reached up and touched my jaw bone, which was surely popping out of the socket from the pain I was bearing.

"Why did you do that, you crazy!" Jules scolded.

She started to move away from me, but I pulled her back.

"Worth it," I told her. "Kiss me and make it feel better?" I joked through deep breaths.

She finally relaxed against me, realizing she wasn't going to win, "no kisses because I'm mad you just hurt yourself again."

I felt a smile touch the corners of my mouth. That sounded like the old Jules.

"Okay, Lil mama."

She turned on her side and used her free hand to draw calming strokes on my chest and stomach with her nails. I closed my eyes, embracing the comfort from the girl I loved.

A couple minutes of cuddling later, noise from the door forced my eyes open. If it was a nurse or doctor, I'd beg them to leave. This was more healing for me than they'd ever know.

But Paige popped her head in.

Seeing that the coast was clear, she ushered the rest of the crew in. I couldn't help but feel proud of the fact that Canyon fit in so seamlessly with the group. He was comfortably chatty away with Ashlie and Smitty.

"So now that we're all in a happy mood and we're all together," Paige said looking around at the group with a bright smile, "Guess what?!" She was wringing her hands in excitement, and she looked like she was about to burst.

"We're pregnant!" Paige called out.

Max's face stretched into the biggest grin I'd ever seen on his face, "it's gonna be a son, I know it!"

Paige rolled her eyes at him and he placed a hand on her stomach.

"This is so exciting!" Ashlie called out.

"Congrats, man," I told Max and I gave a wink to Paige. It was fitting for her to be a mom. "Time for a diaper party, eh?"

I turned to look down at Jules face. She was looking at Paige in a wistful way.. she seemed happy, but I detected a twinge of jealousy, maybe?

I hoped I was still good at reading her because that made me fucking elated.

The group was chatting and not paying attention to us.

I leaned in to whisper in her ear, "Wanna make a baby?"

She pushed me away and gave an eye roll.

"I'm serious," I told her with a straight face. "Do you want to get married and have babies with me?"

Her doubtful expression turned serious.

"You know you wanna…" I teased, bumping her shoulder with mine. "Or we can just have babies and forget the marriage part... but I really wanna give you a ring and my last name."

She looked dumbstruck.

"Did you lose your mind?" She finally asked.

"I mean… my mind is probably fucked… but I do mean it. Actually, wanna be a pregster bride? Not really traditional, but it would really show everybody you're mine," I joked. I leaned in to whisper in her ear again, "mine to love and protect. Forever." I pressed a kiss into her temple. "And I kinda want to now."

She turned her head and kissed me on the mouth.

I laughed against her lips and cringed in pain as she accidentally elbowed me in the ribs.

"Sorry!" She pulled back and looked at me. Tears were starting to form on her bottom eyelids and I started to move her off me.

"What are you doing?" She asked, "These are happy tears!"

"I have to get down on one knee," I grunted.

She pulled at my arm to make me get back in the bed, but it was no use. I was already up and moving.

"Jesus. I got way more beat up for you than hockey," I struggled. "This is gonna be kinda short, okay?"

She laughed through her tears as I bent down in front of her and took her delicate hands. I looked up at her and saw her as a stressed out, lonely teenager with a beautiful smile, a twenty-somethin excited to start life, and as the strongest, kindest mother I could ever know.

"Juju Louise, I've been wanting to do this for over a decade," the truth of those words almost choked me up. "We didn't get it right in our Gametime. But I think we were able to get it right in our Overtime. If we're together, we've really won, baby. Marry me?"

She came closer to me and put both hands behind my head and bent her head to kiss me. Her glassy eyes looked down at me.

"Yes."

EPILOGUE: TJ VONNIE

It was kind of a shocking realization that all the guys around me were starting to get married and have kids. I was one of the youngest in the group… and the only one still actually playing hockey… but still… There had been a change in a lot of the League guys that I played beer hockey with all summer.

I sat back in my fancy white wooden chair and looked out around me. It really was a beautiful place to get married. I'd only ever passed though rinks in Michigan, and had never made it to what they called "up north." They plotted a huge tent, dance floor, and a bunch of tables and chairs right at the base of a lake, and they had a gorgeous summer day. It was perfect for them. Grey had taken Jules outdoor skating up here during a tournament when they were kids I guess.

It was a pretty small wedding. Neither of them had much family. But there were a ton of hockey guys milling around with their girlfriends or dates and pretty much a whole hockey team of little guys belonging to young families- they were probably on Grey's team.

I peered a couple rows in front of me where I saw Max quietly burping a teeny baby boy in a onesie that had a graphic suit printed on it. Jesus. I shook my head. Max topped off his suit with a hat turned backwards. Only he would do that. Actually, I was surprised he wasn't wearing his hockey warm ups. For as much of a goofball he was, he was taking the dad stuff seriously. Anyone could easily tell that he loved daddy duty. He had yet to relinquish the baby to his longtime girlfriend Paige, who's blonde head was next to his.

Grey was up front, waiting for the wedding procession to start. The only person standing next to him was Jules' little son. The kid looked pretty spiffy in a tux with his hair gelled up. But Grey looked like the absolute man. He always was in my mind. He was my idol growing up. I was always watching Grey, Max, and Smitty as a kid. I think all of us younger players were watching them, wanting to be them.

A lot of guys around the rink thought I was Grey's younger brother because I looked so much like him. I was just a little more Italian looking and a couple inches shorter to my disappointment. I'd only made it to 6 foot even. We had the same dark hair and trimmed beard most of the time. I shaved for the event… Grey had not. I think because his fiancé, well, I guess wife starting today, loved it. He claimed she was mad at him every time he shaved.

I took another swig of my beer. I hoped that was allowed. This was my first wedding. I looked around and realized no one else had brought their drinks to the white seats and nearly choked. Shit. I already fucked up. I doubted that Grey would notice, or care if he did, because he was so love struck by Jules. Watching them was kind of nauseating.

The music started then and everyone got to their feet. I was a second slower. I really should've been paying more attention.

Jules came into sight then, and damn. She was so beautiful.

It was kind of weird- I always thought pregnant ladies looked creepy before. But looking at Jules with Grey's future baby in there… It was kind of perfect. She looked hot actually. She was only about six months prego, so no danger of the baby like popping out of her or anything. It was kind of cute.

I felt the urge to reach out and touch her baby bump.

And what the fuck? Like why? I closed my eyes and gave a good head shake. I was probably just more drunk than I realized.

But when I opened my eyes, my judgement didn't change. She was like the hottest woman I'd ever seen. She looked like a fucking angel with her wispy, white dress and baby bump. I was kind of jealous of Grey.

I looked back to the front to see him and his reaction was priceless. I mean, I'm a dude. Like who cares. But it was pretty sweet that such a hardass like Greyson Scott was tearing up.

I was happy for them. At least some people could get it right. I kept trying with no luck. Paige tried to coach me through the last relationship but then she stopped helping because she thought the girl I was after was kind of a bitch. She kind of was. Oh well.

As soon as Jules made it to their altar, Grey lifted her veil, placed both of large hands on either side of her belly and leaned down to kiss her forehead.

I rolled my eyes as the "aww's" I heard escaping from the mouths of practically every female in the audience, but I had to admit, it was kind of nice. It was real. Their love. Everyone could tell by the way they looked at each other.

When the priest finally made it to the ring exchange, Canyon, Jule's son, grabbed the ring out of his tiny jacket pocket and handed it to Grey, which caused the guests to laugh and "aww" again.

After their dramatic kiss, Greyson threw his fist up in triumph and everyone cheered.

I usually didn't come to weddings. I typically just got the invite and threw it in the trash. I didn't like the pressure of having to bring a date and taking the chance that the date could get all weepy or drunk or weird. Like I said, I didn't have much luck when it came to women. But Grey told me I had to come and didn't even give me a plus one.

But without a date I felt kind of awkward during the cocktail hour. I was drinking by myself at a high-top table trying to inconspicuously scope out any single women, but Jules didn't seem to have many single friends.

Until Max finally saved me.

He came by my table and held his baby out to me, practically shoving him in my arms. The pudgy guy had so much drool on him that his onesie was wet down to his belly button.

"Just in case you make it to the Chel too," Max said with a wink and then shot a picture of us. By Chel he meant "NHL." I was still playing a level down in the AHL. He was such a weirdo. Like I wouldn't know his baby for real? I was always around. Max fucking employed me every summer at the rink. But I guess goalies were always kind of weirdos. I was so focused on not dropping his baby that I must've looked kind of weird myself. But if I dropped this baby, he'd kill me. I'd literally be a dead man.

I stared down into the baby's big, happy eyes and was struck with the responsibility. The baby just smiled at me and made a cute noise, showing it's two teeny teeth. How could it smile at me? Did it not realize that I could literally accidentally drop it and hurt it bad?

"He likes you, bud! But, hey, you're kinda gripping him hard," Max said. "Jesus. Give me back my baby." That caused me to relax and laugh a bit, I never thought I'd hear those words from him.

Just as soon as I handed the baby off, extremely carefully, I felt a pat on the back.

I turned to see Grey and Jules making their rounds. I pulled both of them into a quick hug.

"Happy for you, kids," I told them, but I couldn't take my eyes off Jules ' stomach. Right then it moved. It really fucking moved. I felt my eyes pop out of my head at the surprise.

"Jesus, it's really real," I couldn't keep the awe out of my voice. Both of them laughed at me in return and Grey placed a hand on the bump.

"Fuck yeah it is," he said. "We're gonna have more too. Right baby?" He said down to her.

Jules rolled her eyes, but couldn't keep the smile from sliding onto her face. She obviously loved what he said too.

She reached up and patted his face, "Mama's gotta use the bathroom."

"Need help?" Grey said as he wagged his eyebrows, to which she rolled her eyes again.

Grey kept his eyes on her until she reached the tent where a bathroom had been set up.

"I think she's going to be constantly pregnant for the next ten years," Grey joked.

I think love made him lose his ever-loving mind, "Woah there, bud. That's a lot of babies."

"You'll know when you know. But damn. She wants me even more now, like all the time. Pregnancy hormones are amazing."

"I thought pregnant chicks just cried all the time?" I asked him curiously.

"Nope!" Max jumped in and looked at Grey. "Crying only comes after the birth, man- baby, mom, and you too probably. Have fun with that."

Grey shrugged his shoulders, "I can handle it." He turned back to me, "How are you doin, man?"

"Kinda sucks you didn't give me a plus one," I joked.

"We didn't give you a plus one because Jules and I think you'd be great for someone here," Grey said pointedly.

I couldn't help but think they were trying to pull one over on me.

"Okay, I'll bite," I finally said, looking at him skeptically, "Who?"

"That, we aren't going to tell you, bro. We didn't tell her either. If you find each other, great. If not, too bad, so sad," he laughed. "But we do actually think you two would be perfect."

With that he slapped me on the back again before disappearing into the crowd, leaving me to wonder if what he said had any truth to it.

ABOUT THE AUTHOR

As a former competitive figure skater, S.C. Kate grew up in ice rinks and loves it as a setting for her contemporary sports romance stories. She lives in metro-Detroit and still frequents arenas to cheer on her siblings during hockey games.

When not writing, she is obsessed with Dunkin Donuts iced coffee, and traveling around Northern Michigan.

S.C. Kate has one other published sports romance titled, *It Takes a Campus*, available on Amazon, and she is currently busy writing TJ's story for Ice League book 2 (coming soon!).

S.C. loves to hear from her readers. Visit @authorsc_kate on Instragram or @sc_kate on TikTok.

Made in the USA
Las Vegas, NV
21 December 2021